Love and Latkes

Love and Latkes

A Friendships and Festivals Romance

Stacey Agdern

TULE
PUBLISHING

Dedication

This book is dedicated to Dr. James Quinn, who inspired me to be a better writer and a better person. Thank you, Dr. Quinn, for your patience. May you see your heart in Dr. Engleman.

It's also dedicated to Barry Agdern, whose lifelong love of learning inspired my own. I love you, Dad.

Chapter One

T HE SUBJECT LINE of the email burning a hole in Batya Averman's inbox was written in bold.

LATKE FRY-OFF HOSTED by George Gold/Golden Road Productions

She'd sent in her résumé to the town and the production company a few months before on a whim fueled by possibility. She was a good web designer, but she also knew food. Knew it well, especially after building her own website, full of interviews and the kinds of things that might possibly be, for a person with less stage fright, the basis of a television show.

But she couldn't stop dreaming, and maybe, maybe if she could design the website for this event, she could talk to George Gold himself? Ask him some questions. Get some guidance.

Who knew. The man probably wasn't going to give the time of day to a web designer, but being on one of his sets would be educational for sure. If she got the job.

And now, amidst the email that told her she needed to schedule the next dress fitting at the shop designing the bridesmaids' dresses for Anna's wedding in six months, client emails, and random emails from Sarah telling her she was convinced Isaac was going to propose on the first night of Hanukkah, was *The* response.

She held her breath and clicked on it.

To: BAverman@foodworld.com
From: KTakayama@Rivertown.NY.gov

Batya,

I was very pleased to receive your email. And I am absolutely thrilled to offer you the position.

Looking forward to seeing you back in Rivertown,

Kiyoshi
RTQB Alum with Distinction

She clicked the message shut and sighed before putting her head on the kitchen table. "Why?" she asked. "Why the heck is this my life?"

She heard footsteps and looked up to see her aunt. "What's going on?"

Her aunt was in her seventies—bright haired, bright-eyed, and with a mind like a steel trap. She'd come to Hollowville from California five years before because Tante Shelly had needed family. Now she couldn't imagine her adult life without the close relationship she'd built with her aunt.

But a discussion about the mistake she'd made and the past she'd left behind in Rivertown wasn't going to be a comfortable one, even with Tante Shelly.

"Rivertown," she said, hedging just a little bit, "is hosting a latke competition."

Tante Shelly raised an eyebrow, and it was obvious the older woman could see past the story Batya wanted to tell. "I don't understand."

Now she *had* to spill the details, and hope Tante would understand. "I'd read somewhere that George Gold is hosting a latke-making competition in some town," Batya said, feeling like she was driving backward through quicksand. "And, so I sent an inquiry to the committee about doing the website. I didn't realize that the town was Rivertown."

Tante Shelly snickered. "Oh my dear. You know exactly why this is your life?"

"I don't. I mean, I was excited to see how a small town would run a latke-making competition. For abstract, and maybe website purposes, and more importantly as a way of working with George Gold. He's really hands-on for the things he hosts, because he doesn't want his name attached to anything inferior. So I offered my services. Website build, onsite consultation at most hours during the event itself, which I normally offer in conjunction with websites I'm doing for specific pop-up events."

"And you didn't check to see where the competition was

before you offered?"

Which was the part of the story Batya was most embarrassed about. "I'm usually more circumspect about checking the information and locations of places I send my résumé to," she admitted. "But this time I wasn't."

"Why?"

And that was the million-dollar question. "I can work anywhere, you know, and honestly I kinda would for George Gold. I figured it would be California or Florida or somewhere like that, knowing his usual filming trajectory. The last thing in the world I expected was for Rivertown, the village that barely even acknowledged their Jewish population when I lived there, to have a latke competition."

Tante Shelly nodded. "You know, places change, Batya. People change. Towns change. Apparently, the new rabbi at the synagogue has a very different outlook on community outreach than the last one had. And from what I hear, he's got a seat on the council."

"Why do I not believe you?"

"Maybe the other thing you should think about," Tante Shelly continued, shifting into lecture mode, "is that a large number of people come here, to the next town over from Rivertown, to celebrate Hanukkah. Tourist dollars are on the table. And not thinking about those tourists costs Rivertown money. A lot of money."

Batya nodded. "That I believe. And I understand the facts, Tante Shelly, but I just…"

"You just what?"

Batya sighed. "Why, of all places, does it have to be...there?"

Tante Shelly sat down at the table, settled herself in and smiled, her wide hazel eyes soft yet trained directly on her. "*Bashert*, maybe."

Thankfully, Batya wasn't drinking anything; she would have spewed liquid all over her aunt if she had. Instead, she tried to tamp down her sarcasm. "Rivertown is *not* my soul mate."

"No," her tante replied, "but you've been successful at everything life has thrown at you. It's bashert, fated, that you take the next step toward your dreams there. Where you started."

"I didn't start there," Batya replied as if she couldn't get the words out fast enough. "I left there as quickly as possible. You could see the burn marks under my tires as I went across the country."

"Yes, and you didn't return." Tante Shelly smiled. "You know I never thanked you."

"For what?"

"For coming here when I needed you. Thank you."

"There's no reason to thank me," she said, reaching a hand out and placing it over her aunt's wrinkled one. "You needed me; I needed a change. You did everything for me when I was a kid. I adore you, Tante Shelly."

She smiled, and Batya could see that smile was still bittersweet, her uncle's loss still just below her aunt's skin. "I love you, dear," she said. "And I know that it's time for you to take the next step."

"Even if it's going backward?"

"This isn't backward," Tante Shelly said, rubbing her wrist with her thumb. "No, mamaleh. This is forward."

"Forward." Batya tried desperately to hide her disbelief. Yes, building a website for a food competition was a logical next step, but nothing in the world would make her think returning to Rivertown for any reason was moving forward. "Okay."

She opened her email app, then went to Kiyoshi's email and hit reply.

This was happening. Whether she wanted it to or not.

ABE NEWMAN LOCKED the front door to his childhood home.

Two years before, he'd realized that his fire was for barbecue and not the intricate tax work he'd spent so much time poring over. So, he'd sold his Manhattan apartment and moved back to Rivertown, a phrase he never thought he'd say.

Yet here he was, with a house transferred over to him from his recently retired father, which meant bigger space. And that led to a brand-new smoker. And a pellet grill, of course. Definitely a good trade-off for the increase in his commute time—and his increasingly expensive monthly commuter ticket.

Yet another thought he hadn't expected to ever have.

But he'd made his choice, and now he had both the time and space to make more barbecue. Every weekend, for the select number of people who ordered early enough.

And, boy, did they order.

Enough so that he needed an assistant to get through the weekend, which usually meant his friend Artur joined him...as long as he was able to sample some of the day's product at the end of the night.

But as Abe pulled into his friend Leo's driveway, all he thought of was home.

Home for him was really this group of friends he'd had since forever, since his mother died during the summer between fourth and fifth grade and Mrs. Fratelli watched him every afternoon until his father came home from work.

Leo Fratelli, Leo's girl-next-door-turned-wife, Sapna, and his best friend and barbecue assistant Artur Rabinovich, who'd joined the group as a snot-nosed fifth grader newly arrived from Brighton Beach.

They'd been there for his best triumphs and worst moments.

And on Tuesdays, the night both Leo and Sapna had off from their family restaurants, dinner was at their place. Just the four of them.

"So," Leo said as he brought the plate of steaming rice to the table, "you signed up to compete yet?"

He blew out a breath as he finished folding napkins. "I'm not interested in making three rounds of latkes."

"Not even if the winner of the town latke fry-off gets a George Gold mentorship?" Sapna asked as she came out of the kitchen carrying a huge bowl of curry that smelled like heaven.

"George Gold, as in…?"

"Let's walk the golden road," Leo said with a laugh, echoing the famous Meal Network host's catchphrase. "And yes. Gold is from Rivertown, and he is not only mentoring the winner, but he's also hosting the competition."

George Gold was mentoring the winner of the fry off.

That changed everything.

The possibility of having someone like George Gold as a mentor would help him. Because if Abe let himself think about it, backyard barbecue was a means to an end. What he really wanted was to open a Jewish deli that would, in his heart at least, replace Goldbergs, the deli that had closed its Rivertown location three years before.

And having George Gold and that prize money in his corner? Would make the otherwise impossible dream of deli ownership within his reach.

But he didn't say anything like that. Instead, he nodded, having let all of the information sink in. "Latkes, huh?"

"And," Leo quipped, "if your latkes are as good as your

barbecue—"

"Speaking of which," Sapna interjected, "did you?"

Abe nodded. He'd put together a special portion of barbecue for Leo, saved sides for Sapna, wrapped it all up and put it in their fridge. "It's in there."

"Good. You don't deserve my family's best curry without that meal ticket of yours."

He bowed as Leo laughed. "This," Leo said, "is why I love you."

"You love me because I tolerate your unspiced food."

"It is not unspiced." Leo turned to Abe. "And don't bring up the pepper."

"A little horseradish would go a long way," Abe joked.

"When he's not even defending you," Sapna added, her brown eyes twinkling, "you are in deep trouble."

"He never defends me. Ever." Leo shook his head.

"But you love me anyway," Abe said, laughing as Leo led him to the table.

As they were finishing up, the doorbell rang.

Leo and Abe both laughed. "Artur," they said as Sapna got up to open the door.

"Should I let you in?" they heard her ask him.

"No!" he and his best friend yelled, and they nearly doubled over in laughter, playing the same lines they always did.

"So I get to eat the soofganiyot and macaroons I brought all by myself then?"

"Touch one of those," Leo yelled back, "and I will have

your head, Rabinovich."

"I," Sapna said, "will take them myself because these two yahoos don't deserve it."

"What?" Artur said as he came into the room, a bottle of wine and two bags in his hands. Abe could see the exhaustion in his friend's features, the sign of way too many late nights fixing other people's problems. "You didn't spice the food?"

"I didn't make the main," Leo said with a smile. "I made the rice."

"And if you continue to act like this," Sapna said with a smile, "I might not let you make that anymore."

But Abe smiled. They'd been doing this back and forth since they were young. They argued as much as they loved, and it was the most amazing thing to see. "So, Mr. Artur come lately, what did you bring?"

"Nothing for you," Artur said with a smirk, "unless you tell me that, dear God, you did actually sign up for the fry-off."

Did Abe want to do this?

"Oy," Artur interjected. "You didn't sign up. What exactly could convince you that you can do this?"

"You're too good a cook to sit on the sidelines," Leo added, dropping into the conversation. "You have to compete."

Abe took a macaroon from the bag. "Okay. Fine. I'll sign up to be a contestant. Officially."

"Yes," Leo said as he swiped a soofganiyah from the bag, "you make three nights' worth of latkes and you win the competition. And keep me posted."

"I will," Abe confirmed, "prepare to make three nights worth of latkes." He was going to do this. It was going to work.

Artur nodded, seemingly satisfied with the situation. "And I'll come over Saturday afternoon to be your assistant as per usual?"

Abe nodded. "Yes," he said. "Appreciate it."

He was lucky. That he knew. But getting through this competition was certainly going to depend on the roll of the dice.

Chapter Two

T HE NEXT NIGHT, after he got off the train in Rivertown, Abe headed directly to the gourmet market. He had to pick up the things he needed for the weekend's barbecue, and if he were lucky, he'd also be able to catch the vibe of the town's food scene.

He could feel the excitement in the air as he left the store, bags in hand.

Rivertown was a self-contained bubble on its worst days, a united community on its best. George Gold was making everybody excited in a way they hadn't been since Abe had returned.

He headed back outside into the late October air, stopping at his car to drop off his purchases before heading to his next destination. Gerowitz's Kosher Meats sat in the middle of town, one of the few kosher butchers in the area.

Moshe had taken over a few years ago, when his father retired down to Florida.

"Aaah," Moshe said as Abe walked into the store. "My best customer and favorite purveyor of barbecue."

"Hello, my favorite butcher, and my favorite person on

the planet. So, what do you have this week?"

"A great deal as long as you don't decide to enter the *fa-kakta* latke competition."

"What's wrong with the competition?"

Moshe sighed, picked up a cut of beef. "*They* think it's a big holiday. And making a competition out of latkes is their attempt to turn our nice little holiday into a circus."

Abe shrugged. "I figure the event is the big thing, you know? Not the holiday. And people are in Hollowville, next door, and Rivertown needs something for itself."

Moshe pulled out his knife and started to cut. "What is it they say? Two wrongs don't make a right? Adding a second circus to the first gives everybody the wrong idea, you know, about the things that mean something to *us*."

What Moshe said made sense. On the other hand, if there was anybody who'd understand his reasons for entering the competition, it would be Moshe. "You miss Goldbergs?"

Moshe put his knife down. "Do I miss Goldbergs? I miss selling meat to them. I miss the conversations with Aaron Goldberg when I was debating with my father about whether to take over the store or go to culinary school. I miss having that restaurant there for lunch. I miss what it gave us."

Abe blew out a breath, turned away from the desolation he saw on Moshe's face. And steadied himself. "So," he managed, despite the sweating hands and nerves. "I'm going to try to do the latke competition. If I win, I'm going to use the prize money to fill the space Goldbergs left. Somehow."

"Well then," Moshe replied with a smile. "That fakakta competition would be doing some good. I have faith in this idea of yours."

"Thank you?"

"Thank me by giving me some of your best pulled beef for post Havdalah dinner, hm?"

"Count on it."

After he left the shop, Abe sat down on the bench just outside. In the October air, he pulled out his phone and officially signed up.

≫≫≫⋘⋘⋘

THE LAST TIME she'd left Rivertown, Batya was seventeen, running away from a graduation party confession of love gone bad. The boy she'd had a crush on for four years of high school could only manage one word when she told him how she felt.

"No," he'd said.

Her closest friends had seen him before she did. There were whispers that he and his friends were drinking, that he'd had a few beers before he saw her, but she didn't care. It didn't matter.

The damage had been done.

She was already leaving for California for school in August, and moving up the departure date was easy for an embarrassed seventeen-year-old. It was even easier to stay in

California as someone who desperately wanted to hide from the person she'd been on the other side of the country. Easier still to stay away because Rivertown was a bubble. You lived there, you went to school there. You shopped there, you ate there, and you went to services there. You could spend your entire life in a town like Rivertown and not even know there was a world less than three miles away from the town square.

It was a common joke for people from the city to say "my passport expired" when asked to go to another borough to the north or south, or even to a different neighborhood.

But the real passport?

That was the one you had to engage when you were going between Westchester towns not united by a common school district.

Like Rivertown and Hollowville.

Which is why Hollowville had been safe for Batya; her aunt had needed her and because of Rivertown's bubble—and for that matter Hollowville's—she came.

But now?

One moment of weakness involving a dream of working in television, one opportunity to possibly work alongside George Gold, one silly application, followed by one ridiculous request from her snowbird parents. All of those things combined to mean she was going back.

To Rivertown.

But she wasn't ready; nothing in the world would help her get ready.

She had postponed, procrastinated, and when it came down to it, done everything she could to avoid sending the message, the one where she told her Rivertown friends that she was coming back.

She was a coward.

Fine.

She pulled herself together and sent a text to Claire, Sapna, and Artur. It didn't take even five minutes for her to get pulled into a group chat, as the entire former Rivertown quiz bowl team had to express their opinions.

Their excitement.

S: When will you be back?

C: We need to make dinner a celebration! But we need a thing!

Their relationship had been relegated to random emails, infrequent gatherings in the city or a few trips to California, as well as a holiday card or two. Yet the first sign of her pending arrival in Rivertown was greeted with deep and sincere enthusiasm. She was so, so lucky.

Because when Batya thought about what this group meant to her, the way they so kindly and understandingly dealt with her and her absence over the years, she knew she was stuck. There was no other option. She had to go out with *all* of them.

She opened her planner, turned to her to-do list, and tried to figure out how long it would take her to wrap up everything she had on her plate.

B: I can meet you guys for dinner Thursday night, okay?

L: TOMORROW!!

S: :D

C: Yesssss!

And of course Sapna's husband, Leo, had to chime in.

And wherever Leo and Artur went, so did *he*.

Abe.

The one responsible for her leaving in the first place.

It was better to not think of him in any way. A former crush, a current nightmare. Better that Abe Newman stay far away from her life. Even thinking of him left her both excited and horrified at the same time.

Which was not helpful to consider as she drove through the town she'd spent the past three years in, down the central county thoroughfare, before turning into the town she'd spent more than ten years hiding from.

Driving up the hill, past landmarks she'd spent years trying to forget was hard. She gripped the steering wheel, and as she continued down the road, the changes she saw made her feel more uncomfortable, although she'd expected the inevitable changes would have made her feel better about staying away.

This wasn't going home, she knew. This was a bump in the road, a means to an end. She wasn't going to Rivertown to fix her past. She was going to Rivertown to build a website for a cooking competition and help it succeed.

And maybe get some tips from George Gold about how to bring her career to the next level. Whatever that would be.

She shook her head as she pulled into the driveway.

The old *familiar* driveway that desperately needed to be repaved despite her mother's insistence that it was okay. Yet she had to slow down to practically nothing in order to drive up the path.

As Batya turned off the car, she sat back against the driver's seat and stared at the stone front and glass windows. She'd spent her childhood in this house. It was a refuge for sure, but it wasn't home.

She blew out a breath.

It was going to be okay.

Why she'd actually told her parents she'd do this, she had no idea. But now she was here, she had no other option but to unlock the car door, and step out into the cool bite of fall. And no sooner had her feet hit the gravel than the phone rang.

"You find the key okay?"

The soft sound of her mother's voice made her smile. "Haven't looked yet," she said, "but I'm here."

"Good to hear you made it. Now listen, if you have any trouble, you give us a call."

"Why should I bother you in your snowbird paradise with problems in Rivertown?"

"Because we know who to call," her mother pointed out. "You know, if you have a problem."

All the people who need to be called. If you have a problem.

The electrician, the carpenter, the repair person who did work on the appliances, the plumber. And the alarm company.

"Don't you have all that information in the office, in that folder?"

"Yes, but still."

She blew out a breath. She could do this.

Not to mention, the grocery order she'd made should be coming shortly. Which meant she had to get inside and get settled.

"Thanks for calling," she said. "Love you."

"Call me later," her mother replied. "Love you too."

After ending the call, she got out of the car, heading towards the house and the next chapter of her life.

Chapter Three

THE CONSTANT BUZZING of the group chat made it impossible for Abe to concentrate.

He adored his quiz bowl buddies, but it was really enough.

He, too, was excited that Batya was coming back to Rivertown. But the excitement was just...

Overwhelming.

He had way too much on his plate to let his mind rest on her. On seeing her again for the first time in a long time.

Such a long time, in fact, that it was quantified by multiples of ten.

Not since the final graduation party where he'd completely messed up.

Because despite what the Hollywood teen movie industry might have audiences believe, not every high school graduation party crush admission ended well. Especially if, after having your first few beers, you managed to slur in a way that made you incapable of telling the girl you reciprocated her feelings.

Like he had.

And now, after a long day of organizing documents that had come in from one of Lieb Waxman's wealthiest clients, he headed to Grand Central and the loud car on the express train to Rivertown.

There were, in fact, three different messages, waiting for him in the group chat.

Artur: Don't tell me you're not coming.

Leo: Don't make me have to leave the kitchen and drag you here by the collar.

He sighed, texted:

Abe: I'm on the train. I'll be there when I get there. It's not far from the train station.

Leo: This place hasn't moved in fifty years. Still up the street from the RTS.

Artur: You have a car there?

Abe smiled. Ahh, Artur.

Abe: I do. Thanks though.

Thankfully, that put an end to the messages, so he was able to sit back against the seat of the train. He looked out the window, following the Hudson, the river from where Rivertown got its name.

But he couldn't relax, not like usual.

There was something in the air, only this time, he knew the something had a name.

Batya Averman.

This was going to be a long night.

BATYA WAS NOT ready for this.

She could wait a million years and not be ready.

She wanted to see the members of the quiz bowl team and celebrate their joys.

She just didn't want to see Abe. In fact, she'd be much happier to leave him in her past. What was it Anna had said about her now fiancé? That they had emotional baggage between them.

Yep. That was it. And the emotional baggage that sat between her and Abe was the sort Batya had no desire to revisit. Except she was on her way to a dinner she couldn't get out of, even if she wanted to.

"You're heeere!" Claire squeezed her the second she came into view. She adored Claire and her exuberance most of the time but this was…a lot.

"Oh my God, *Batya*. You are not an illusion!" Sapna too, wanted in on the group hug, which was fine. Because she *missed* Sapna.

"Did you get the thing I sent you for Nicola?"

"She destroyed it in seconds, even though it was gorgeous. Leo found it and the destruction hilarious though."

"I'll bet," Batya said, grinning.

"Come on," Sapna said, gesturing at the group. "I don't know about you, but I've been on my feet all day running after a two-year-old."

"Who's missing?" Claire asked.

"Leo's on tonight behind the scenes."

Batya nodded. This had been Leo's family's restaurant when she'd lived in Rivertown, and despite his father's best and most fervent wishes, Leo had apparently taken it over. Complete with his Ivy League hospitality degree.

"Kiyoshi," Claire said, "who's running late as usual and will probably end up canceling, Artur, and Abe."

Batya tried not to think about the fact that Abe was expected and hadn't arrived. Maybe he'd miss this.

"Not Abe," Sapna said. "Artur *actually offered to* pick him up at the train station, so you get an idea of how this is going."

"Artur doesn't drive anybody," Claire confirmed. "Because that would require someone actually messing up the inside of his car.

Batya snickered. "Yes, that's the Artur I remember. Same person, different car, same obsession."

"But," Sapna said, "my guess is that he's hovering outside, in the parking lot, prepared to herd Abe up here by hook or by crook."

Drama already and not everybody was here. If nothing else, Batya had to be thankful for that. Especially since later or pending arrivals gave her necessary time with her friends.

Claire bit her lip. "Do we have the restaurant to ourselves?"

"I believe so," Sapna said. "At least the room we're in."

Batya grinned. This she could deal with. "Let's do this," she said.

WHEN THE TRAIN arrived at the Rivertown station, Abe followed the herd of commuters into the parking lot.

He unlocked the car and got in, waiting his turn to drive up the street to Fratelli's. Hopefully, there would be a parking space, because Rivertown and parking spaces never went well together.

Ever.

When he pulled into the parking lot, he could see the familiar cars; the ones that usually heralded the quiz bowl group. He pulled into a spot near Artur.

And unfortunately, or fortunately for him, his friend was waiting. "What took you so long?"

"Some people don't have fungible schedules," Abe joked. "Some people don't set their own hours."

"Well," his friend replied with a laugh, "setting your own schedule doesn't do anything when you get called at two a.m. to help fix someone's problem."

"One of the many reasons I am very glad I don't have your job."

"And," Artur quipped, "numbers terrify me, so I am equally joyous about not having yours. But…"

There was always a *but* with Artur. "What? I'm listening."

"You're going to have to be careful. Like very much so."

Abe raised an eyebrow. "And why is that?"

"Sapna says that Batya is here already."

"I see," he said.

"No. You don't. You have to roll with the punches, follow the current and all of the metaphoric stuff."

"More than usual?"

Artur nodded. "Yep. Much more than usual."

Now Abe understood what Artur meant. The words Abe had messed up years before would serve as the lens through which he and Batya would always see their relationship. She'd be wary of him.

He hated that.

At some point, he'd tell her he'd been drunk the night of the graduation party. That the beer had stolen his ability to tell her he'd reciprocated her feelings.

But that would mean he'd have to talk to her in a way that didn't scare her for once.

And as he followed Artur into the restaurant, he wondered if that was going to be possible.

THE NIGHT WAS going rather swimmingly, if Batya had to say so herself. The chairs were comfortable, and the jokes were flowing.

It had been so long since she'd seen them all in person like this, and yet it felt as if their last meeting had been only yesterday.

The food was amazing as well. Leo had made them all a feast.

She was dipping a mozzarella stick into his family's famous secret recipe marinara sauce when the door opened.

It was Abe, of course. Abe and Artur.

"Batya!"

Sapna's voice broke into the silence, and she turned toward her friend.

Her friend was gesturing sharply toward the table and the bowl and the…

Oh.

Which was a seriously inconvenient time to remember the mozzarella stick, her shirt and the sauce. As if it were a bit of slow-motion movie mastery, like one of those commercials for bleach, Batya could see the sauce spill out of the dish, the bright red marinara flowing and moving like a tidal wave, heading toward the white tablecloth.

Her "no" echoed in the silence. She reached for her napkin but somehow managed to drop her sweater into the red sauce.

She wanted to cry, to hide under her chair, but it wasn't

happening.

Two minutes back in Rivertown, with Abe, and it was as if she'd never left.

Ugh.

"It's fine, Batya."

Abe. Sounding completely dismissive and either unaware of or ignoring her embarrassment.

"I'll take the stuff to the dry cleaners and order a round of mozzarella sticks for the table. It's my fault for showing up late like this."

She'd spent most of her life trying to analyze Abe, but she wouldn't do it now. She wouldn't stare into his eyes, wondering if he'd ever look at her as more than the embarrassing one with the weird name. Because, unfortunately, that analysis never went well. Ever. She also had to remember that being covered in marinara sauce wasn't exactly that attractive.

"It's fine," she said, trying to be as nonchalant about this as she possibly could. "I'll take care of it. All I need is a bleach marker and it'll be fine. I don't need a production or a dry cleaners, but thank you for the offer."

"I've got a bleach marker," Sapna said from the opposite side of the table, breaking into her thoughts. "This is what happens when you live with a two-year-old."

Batya smiled, but she didn't feel that smile, not at all.

"Thanks," she said. At least she had friends who were capable of heading off an embarrassing incident before it got worse.

As GOOD AS he was with people, Abe always managed to do the wrong thing around Batya.

He was cool, relaxed, even funny at times. Yet around her, he turned into a complete wet fish.

And that was being nice about it.

"Yeah," he said, sitting back against the chair, answering Claire's question about his week. "This week has been ridiculous at work. Just got a box of documents for the independent republic."

Batya raised an eyebrow. "Independent republic?"

Abe nodded. "Firm's got an extremely wealthy client, with holdings about as vast as an independent republic. Came to us because they insist on paying every single bit of the taxes they owe, which is both rare and makes things complex. So we start early."

"Interesting," she said.

Was she judging him?

"Very interesting."

She was absolutely judging him.

He smiled. "Hard work, good reasons. Anyway."

"Do you know what you're making this weekend?"

Ahhh, Artur. Savior of the moment. "Beef, courtesy of Moshe the magician, and a good strong rub, courtesy of my own two hands, and then smoke it with my favorite chips, courtesy of Fitzgerald's tree farm."

"When do you set up orders for this week?"

Batya again raised an eyebrow, and he wondered what she'd look like, sitting in his kitchen, watching him put together his smoker and prep the orders for pickup. But then he smiled, sat back. "Set up the smoker before I head off to work on Friday, open everything Saturday night, and people pick up then."

"I want chicken. Why won't you make me chicken, Abe?" Claire asked, grinning back at Batya. "Come on."

"I can do chicken next week."

"You said that three weeks ago."

"Chicken is boring," Abe said. "But if we're doing chicken, it's twice the work because there are both different rubs and different specialties for chicken."

And as he settled back into the familiar conversations, remembering at each moment that he was expected to be on good behavior, he wondered if he'd ever feel comfortable around Batya. Or if she'd ever feel comfortable around him.

Chapter Four

T HE NEXT MORNING, Batya was drinking her coffee, making notes, when she got an email from Kiyoshi summoning her to his office for a conversation about the competition.

Time never waited for anybody, so she jumped into the shower, attempted to make her curls look coherent with the application of a few fingers, some gel and a prayer or two, and put on clothing appropriate for a meeting at town hall.

Of all places.

Kiyoshi had been a few years older than her group of quiz bowl friends, a junior who competed on the varsity quiz bowl team when they were all freshmen. He'd been a good guy, a good mentor. She also remembered that when he'd graduated, he'd intended to study something about cities. Only to come back and work *here*, having married the object of his high school crush, one Lilly Mendelowitz, who she'd known at Schecter.

Apparently, there was something about Rivertown that never let residents leave permanently.

But Batya wasn't going to a meeting with Kiyoshi to talk

about old high school memories or stupid decisions she'd once made.

Nope. She was going to town hall, with its multistory façade, the tall steeple-like bell tower at the top, and the front that reminded her in some strange way of Rockliffe—Anna's fiancé's family home.

And nope. She was not going to think about governmental buildings and the fact that one of her best friends was marrying a guy who grew up in a house that dwarfed the size of a government building.

Nope.

She was here to talk business. Her business. The website.

And maybe try to get some information from Kiyoshi about George Gold.

Her own agenda clear in her mind, she parked in a lot nearby and headed into the building. She followed the directions the security guard gave her until she came to a door marked K. Takayama.

She knocked and stepped into the office.

Kiyoshi's dark hair was brushed back, his brown eyes twinkling back at her. He was still a fastidious dresser, his suit as impeccable as the outfits she remembered seeing him wear in high school.

"Interesting, hm?"

She laughed. Apparently his sense of humor hadn't changed either. "Yes. Very interesting."

"In a good way or a bad way?"

"I think," she said as she settled down into the chair in front of his desk, "it's in an interesting way. You wanted to learn about city structure, planning for cities; now you're using it here."

"I figure a town like Rivertown deserves a chance at having people who aren't afraid of change working on the inside."

"Fair enough. So speaking of change," she said. "What kind of website are you looking for, for the competition?"

Kiyoshi shrugged. "Don't know really." He pulled out a binder and passed it over. "You've done some great work," he said. "I really like the Hanukkah festival website."

"You know I'm not going to give you the festival website, right?"

Kiyoshi nodded. "I know that. And I don't think the council wants that. What I think it does want is a website that best reflects the kind of story we're telling. We're not hosting a festival. We're hosting a competition."

Batya nodded, scratching a few notes on her notepad.

"Do you know the specifics of the format?"

"Three nights, three rounds, each an elimination round. One winner at the end."

"Is there going to be a theme for each one? Special ingredients?"

"They are considering that, but they may decide otherwise. You should talk to Linda, George Gold's assistant. We don't know what they're going to do."

Batya nodded. From what she knew of him, she could tell that George Gold really enjoyed making competitions of his own, and each of the shows he hosted had really fun details. "Okay. I'll send Linda an email."

"Good." He paused. "You should also go see Dr. Engleman. Email him and let him know you're here."

Batya beamed. She hadn't seen their high school quiz bowl advisor in way too long. "I absolutely will."

"Excellent," Kiyoshi said with a smile. "Glad to have you back in town."

She smiled. "It's good to see you in person."

Kiyoshi laughed. "I get it. I totally get it. You're not back in that traditional sense." And then he paused. "You know," he said, "not every single memory you associate with this place should be bad."

"Bad memories are like weeds," she said. "Too many of them overwhelming everything everywhere."

Kiyoshi nodded. "Speaking of which, I'm sorry I didn't make dinner last night. Your quiz bowl year group is a great one and, like I told Sapna and Leo, you guys needed last night on your own. Also, you're technically working for me now, and I don't want to make it weird."

"Understood," she replied. "And thank you, by the way."

Kiyoshi smiled. "You're welcome."

ABE PACED HIS office.

Now that he'd entered the competition, he had just weeks to make and test a reliable latke recipe he could prepare with his eyes closed, if the room he was in lost power, or was set on fire.

Piece of cake.

Of course, none of that was going to happen if he didn't get some more time. Late nights at work, barbecue on the weekend…when was he going to find time to make latkes and the applesauce he'd need?

Which meant, as he told Artur on the train from Rivertown that morning, "I have no choice."

"Think of it this way," his friend had replied. "You're taking your latke frying to the next level and actually doing something for yourself."

Which made sense.

It was way past time for him to make this move. The first thing he did was leave his office. And as certain sorts of news was best delivered in person, his destination lay just beyond the double doors that separated Lieb Waxman Tax LLC's founder Hyman Lieb's office from the rest of the firm.

Lieb's secretary nodded, and Abe knocked at the door.

"Come in," Lieb said.

He opened the door, only to catch the firm's eighty-year-old elder statesman attempting to hide the wrappers from the chocolate gelt he'd been eating. "Sorry to interrupt."

Lieb laughed as he gestured toward the chair that sat in

front of his desk. "No interruption. Come in, sit down. What can I do you for?"

"Well," Abe began, "I realize that there's a procedure for these things, but I didn't want to start it without talking to you first, because of some of the projects I've been working on."

"Tell it to me straight. You going somewhere else?"

"Nope. Just wanting to take some time, maybe lower my in-person hours until after Hanukkah."

Lieb, the one who'd been ordering enough to help support his barbecue for years in its various incarnations, looked at him as if he couldn't believe what Abe had just said. "Hanukkah? I'd be less curious if we were talking about other holidays. What's going on?"

He blew out a breath. "I'm going to participate in a cooking competition, and I need to lessen my in-person hours."

"Do you have a plan, a schedule? Because I am interested in a cooking competition that you'd be participating in around Hanukkah time." He paused. "Unless it's just latkes."

Abe shrugged. "I think it's just latkes, but it's supposed to be hosted by George Gold, so it's never just latkes."

"You're doing that Rivertown one?"

Abe nodded. "I'm from Rivertown, so I kinda feel somewhat obligated, you know?"

He had no idea what to expect from his boss, but the smile was unmistakable, the light in his eyes was bright. "Go fully virtual," Mr. Lieb said. "I'll also temporarily lessen your workload, too. Not the independent republic, of course, because you're the best at that. Also, I have a proposition for you."

Abe raised an eyebrow. "I'm listening."

"If you want the firm to sponsor you in any way, let me know."

He blinked. "Sponsorships?"

Lieb laughed. "My wife was watching one of those Christmas movies, and it was a gingerbread competition. A real estate firm sponsored one of the competitors, and I thought that was fakakta. But when you come to me? I say this is good business. Good community work, you know."

And that would be something wonderful. He could get the firm to sponsor him, and that would allow him to do more, maybe increase his budget. Get some extra supplies.

And maybe…

But he couldn't get ahead of himself. "Well," he said, "I would definitely appreciate that. We can talk details once I know better what I would need."

Lieb grinned, his cheeks reddening. "I can't wait to tell my wife that the fakakta movie gave me a business idea. But yes, Abraham. Write up the paperwork, send it to my secretary by close of business today, and you can start teleworking Monday."

Abe left Lieb's office with a spring in his step. Within seconds after submitting his paperwork, he got an email letting him know his request had been approved. It was as if a weight had been lifted off of his shoulders, and he couldn't wait to get started.

>>>><<<<

BATYA STAYED IN town after the meeting, intending to get a handle on what the local restaurant scene looked like.

Tiny was what it was.

So many of the restaurants she'd spent hours in when she was young were gone. She hadn't kept track of the local economy or the change in local tastes, but it hurt all the same. The fact that both Leo and Sapna's family restaurants were still open seemed like unbelievable miracles in this situation. But the closure that hurt the most? Goldbergs.

Of course, Anna could bring her Goldbergs from Long Island, or Batya could even drag herself to Rockliffe Manor to eat there. But apparently gentilification was strong. Although here, in Rivertown, the development cut was wider than just the Jewish shops.

Needing a breather, she walked into the Taj and was seated at a table for lunch.

"So," Batya said as Sapna came out to join her, "talk to me about restaurants here."

Sapna sighed. "Part of the reason why they're doing a cooking competition is to bring more restaurants back to Rivertown. Because the restaurant scene here has been hard.

Difficult."

"Are you on the committee?"

Sapna shrugged. "Leo and I were both involved in the original group of restaurant owners who tried to get the council to do something, but things got a bit nuts for us, so we had to back out. Thankfully, by the time we needed to stop, George Gold was stepping in."

"How did this start?"

"I guess when George came back for a visit, he saw that a lot of restaurants were closing, and he wanted to do something to help. The council was already grappling with what to do about both the Restaurant owner's proposal and Hanukkah, when George heard about both ideas and said yes. Hence the fry-off."

Now the fact that Rivertown was hosting a fry-off made a lot more sense to Batya; it had been George's idea, combining the two proposals on the council's plate. Not the town council's. "Which means," Batya continued, "the goal of all of this is to bring foodies to Rivertown and maybe get a few restaurants here out of the deal?"

Sapna grinned. "That's about how the cookie crumbles."

Batya snickered. "And how's it going?"

"Things are going well with the fry-off, I think. People have signed up to compete."

"Was that before the council announced George was spearheading the whole thing, or after?"

"I mean," Sapna said as she took a sip of her lassi, "there

was local interest before. You know how Rivertown is."

Batya knew all too well about the random conversations where the various organizations, including the shul, debated the merits of involving themselves in council business over an extended series of meetings before all of them did...nothing. Until one of the other organizations stepped up, or the town council announced an incentive. "I do," she said, the conversations over countless dinners where her parents talked about the internal workings of the shul along with the main course coming to mind.

"Anyway," Sapna continued, "once George wanted in, more people stepped up. Keeping up with the neighbors and wanting to rub elbows with George, hm?"

Batya swiped a piece of naan, savoring the taste. "I do know."

"Especially when they learned it was going to be on television."

"Oh, Rivertown," Batya said, shaking her head. "Never change. But in all seriousness, I'm really excited to be a part of it. To tell the story."

"I'm glad you're back," Sapna said with a smile. "But I definitely think you'll like your lunch more."

And if there was nothing else she knew about being in Rivertown, she knew she could trust in Sapna's food.

Chapter Five

RIVERTOWN WAS GORGEOUS in the late fall. The leaves were in full autumn bloom as they prepared to fall from the trees, the colors were bright, and the weather was just perfect. And, Abe noted as he checked his watch, he was up early enough to run to the farmers' market before Artur arrived to help him prep the barbecue.

Coffee in hand, he meandered his way in.

The fall senses, the smell of cinnamon and apples, the sight of pumpkins, made him gleeful. Hmmm, maybe a cinnamon rub?

He stopped at his favorite spice stand and picked up some cinnamon as well as some sage. Next, he went to his favorite produce stand where he bought a bunch of apples, only to turn around and see Batya.

He couldn't take his eyes off of her. Curls, confidence, almost basking in the sun.

And the box she carried had the familiar PieWorks stamp.

Even better.

"Pumpkin pie brings everybody together, I guess."

"Not everybody," he said. "I mean…"

"Right," she said with a bittersweet smile. "You don't like pumpkin pie because you have a texture—"

He shook his head. That was just the excuse he'd given all those years ago when there'd been only one piece left in the pan. "No. I don't have a texture issue. I have a *friend* issue."

"You make no sense, Abe Newman," she said. "I—"

And then the alarm on his watch went off. He swore, in Yiddish of course. "Gotta go." He paused, sorry to leave the moment they were having behind. Sorry to have to deal with the obligation.

But that was the life he wanted, right?

"Time to make the barbecue," he said.

Her smile was welcome. "It's always time to make the barbecue," she replied. "Unless you're, you know, not doing it."

"I have no idea what you mean," he said. "But it was nice to see you."

Nice. Nice to have a conversation with her. Nice to talk.

She nodded, half focused on the pie, half focused on his face. "Yeah. So, maybe I'll order?"

"I'm…I…" He stopped. Pulled himself together. Kept himself from explaining that she didn't have to, that all she had to do was ask. But he didn't think she was ready to hear that, let alone believe it. "I'd like that," he said.

And when he left, he had a pang—whether in his heart,

his stomach, or his head, he couldn't tell—of what could have been if he'd been smart enough to avoid the beer and tell her what he'd felt all those years ago.

But he couldn't go back. No time machine, no back-tracking. Instead, he soothed his heart with music and the prospect of dinner.

And maybe, someday, making hers.

>>>><<<<

As BATYA NAVIGATED the traffic on Route 9, she found herself very, very glad that the pie she'd lovingly placed on the floor of the back seat couldn't respond to the conversation she was having.

At least, couldn't respond to her recriminations.

What was she thinking?

Because not two minutes after leaving the farmers' market, she was replaying the conversation she'd had with Abe in her head. Pondering tone and narrative frame by frame, as if she were a cinematographer.

Why was she doing this to herself?

It's always time to make the barbecue.

Why was she so inarticulate around him? Why couldn't she say something not only coherent but fun?

He'd made a joke, and she'd completely flubbed her response. And there was absolutely no reason.

None, she decided as she pulled into a spot in front of

Tante's apartment building. Absolutely none.

But this was Saturday, and she was in Hollowville to rest and to join her tante for a Shabbas lunch.

Not drown her sorrows in pumpkin pie and whine to Tante Shelly about the obvious reappearance of a crush she'd thought long dead.

Chapter Six

IN GENERAL, ABE enjoyed working from home, pondering ideas for recipes and thoughts on his tax work. But Tuesday morning, Abe realized he had a problem.

There was not enough food in the house. When he was commuting, he had a routine. Coffee in the morning, grab a roll at the train station, grab lunch in the city, meet friends for dinner before spending the weekend cooking, only to begin the cycle again.

And so, trusted cup of coffee by his side, he got into his car, and drove down the hill to Route 9. Which of course, was a mess, as it always was in the morning. But unlike every other morning in his lifetime, he didn't have to worry about getting anywhere specific by any particular time.

Finally, he made the right turn into the parking lot, just beyond the bridge and the Hollowville border. He found a space, and made his way to the local outpost of Baum's Bagels.

Aaaah, Baum's.

Best bagels in the city and he didn't have to go all the way to the city to get them.

The early November chill braced him as he crossed the parking lot, and the shop's metal door handle chilled his palm as he pulled it open. Of course, the bells rang overhead as he crossed the threshold.

There weren't that many people here, thankfully. Not that he had any place to go, but still. As he looked at the menu, his mouth watered and his stomach growled.

As he got closer to the front of the line, he heard the bell ring again, followed by familiar footsteps and the sound of a familiar voice.

Batya was also getting bagels.

Of course she was.

He wasn't surprised though; Baum's was the place everybody went for bagels after Saturday morning shul, the place where the numbers rose by multiples of ten after noon, where the lines ran out the door before Yom Kippur and before the end of Passover. The place the Rivertown Synagogue catering director had on speed dial. This was *the* place and had been for years. If he turned around, he'd recognize three people he knew from shul, at minimum, at any hour of the day.

And the person directly behind him was either on a phone call or typing away on a notes app. The very last thing he wanted to do was surprise Batya, so he waited to say something.

"What is this?" she said, looking up from her phone with a laugh, as if she'd just noticed he was there. "Are you following me?"

"I'm the one who got here first," he said with a smile, "so *if* anybody was following anybody, you'd be the one following me."

"True," she replied.

"But, this is tradition," he said, appealing to her interest in Jewish food history in an attempt to drag them both away from some kind of precipice. "Even if this outpost is the newest, the traditions and the recipes are the same as the one on the lower east side."

"Absolutely," she said, a bit more relaxed. "Bagels aren't just comfort breakfast food. They're history, one of the few Ashkenazi foods brought over…" She stopped, and he saw the slight blush rise in her cheeks. "You don't want to hear me babble about bagels."

"Considering I opened the door, you shouldn't be surprised at the fact I'm interested in listening to you." He paused, looked away from her, before turning back toward her. "And this place is still a huge staple of life in Rivertown."

"Which is all well and good, but…"

Following the gesture, he realized that the number of people that separated them from the front counter had steadily dwindled. As they walked toward the counter, he had a ridiculous idea.

He'd once bought bagels for the entire quiz bowl team to hide the fact that he wanted to buy her breakfast on her birthday.

Which was a stupid idea, but it had worked. Then, she'd ordered a cinnamon raisin bagel with cinnamon cream cheese, the cinnamon flavor of both so strong that he couldn't get the smell out of his old junker of a car for a week.

He hadn't bought her a bagel in years though, not after that and not after…well.

"Same order?"

Batya blinked. "From when? From when I thought the only flavor worth eating on a bagel was cinnamon?"

"Yeah."

"I was seventeen and rebellious, so no."

"So, what then?"

"You really don't have to buy me breakfast because we both appreciate a good bagel and a good bagel shop. It's fine."

"Can *someone* order already?" inquired the clerk behind the counter.

Batya shook her head and then made a noise he couldn't decipher. Surrender? Relief?

"Cinnamon raisin bagel," she said, "toasted. Plain cream cheese, lox, and whitefish, please, and a large coffee." And then she turned to him. "If you're paying, go ahead."

He wasn't sure why she'd changed her mind; was it the clerk's impatience, the certainty of her order or some other intangible?

But he was absolutely not going to look a gift horse in the mouth. "Let me add," he said, "an everything bagel toasted, plain cream cheese, lox, and whitefish, and a large coffee."

And that, if nothing else was a victory. "So what's your plan?"

Why he thought asking that question was a good idea, he'd never know. He'd take it back in an instant, but as that wasn't possible, he resigned himself to not getting an answer. Instead, he focused on the cashier, waiting to pass over his credit card.

But as Batya took her bag and her coffee, she smiled. "I'm going to thank you for my breakfast, get in my car, and drive to the theatre where they're staging the second two rounds of the fry-off. I want to get a sense of what they're doing." She paused. "Are you on the committee or just interested in my schedule?"

"Recently inked competitor," he replied with a smile. "But also, just asking. Maybe volunteering to come with you if you want."

"No. I don't, actually. I do this kind of site reconnaissance better on my own."

"Very well then," he said. And then having nothing else he could say to her that would make her understand him, he went with a classic. "Have a good day."

"Thank you for my breakfast," she said as she settled the bag in one arm and the coffee in the other, "and I'll see you around."

And that was an ending if he'd ever heard one, so he didn't follow her out of the shop. He just let her go.

﹥﹥﹥≪﹤﹤

BATYA FELT PROUD of herself as she drove to the theatre. She'd managed to, once again, survive an encounter with Abe that didn't involve spilling anything on him or making a complete *draikopf* of herself in front of everybody who'd come into Baum's that morning.

Then again, she hadn't been holding any liquids. Or anything breakable. She was...calm.

Even though her heart beat faster as she drove along main street.

Ugh.

Less than a week in Rivertown and she was already reverting to a teenager with a crush.

If you're paying, go ahead.

If she'd been winking, eyelashes dripping in mascara, she could have been just a little bit more obvious. One second of his smile and she folded like a cheap suit.

She needed to stop analyzing her response to him or she'd end up doing something worse. *Like panning for emotional gold in his responses and gestures.*

Batya banged the steering wheel, narrowly avoiding the horn. *I am not doing this to myself again*, she swore as she pulled into a parking space in front of the theatre. She was a professional and an adult, here on a website design job, and she needed to act like it.

She got out of the car, heading up the front stairs of the theatre. Her appointment with Dr. Engleman and then Linda, George Gold's assistant, was at 10:00 a.m. and she was on time, which was about the best she could say for herself.

"If these walls had ears," said a familiar voice.

She turned to see her quiz bowl advisor and her favorite English teacher. Graying dark hair, thick-rimmed glasses, and a smile brighter than the sun. "Dr. Engleman," she said with a smile. "So glad to see you here."

"Batya Averman, as I live and breathe. I'm always thrilled to see your face. Even though I haven't had that privilege very often in the last few years."

She nodded. "I know. And I appreciate you. So much."

"Oh," he said, his eyes sparkling behind his glasses. "I was always proud of you. I am proud of you."

She smiled. "I'm very glad to hear that."

"So what brings you to this beautiful theatre?"

"I'm making the website for the fry-off," she said. "Getting to know the staging area."

"Well," he said, "let's just take a bit of a tour, hmm?"

She took out her phone, prepared to take pictures of the setup. "I'm excited to put this together, tell the story."

"And I assume you're going to tell more stories on that

LOVE AND LATKES

other website of yours?"

"You read my food site?"

"Of course I do," he replied, his smile indulgent. "I told you I was *proud* of you. You just assumed you knew what I was proud *about*."

She laughed. "Fair enough," she said. "So are you on the council?"

"Oh no," he said. "They figured they'd need someone to either be a sideline reporter or a liaison to George. He chose the sideline because he liked the local angle, so here I am."

"That's so amazing," she said with another smile as she snapped a photo of the fry-off's logo as it sat against the stage.

"Well," he replied, "it should be a fun thing, and help-ful."

"Yeah." She sighed. "The restaurants here. It's been hard to see they were gone."

She could see Dr. Engleman's uneasy shrug out of the corner of her eye. "Change is hard; life is hard. Things happen, and people step up to help or they don't."

Batya nodded as she continued to take photos.

"You know," Dr. Engleman said in the silence that had sprung up between them, "I see all the equipment, but nobody's here."

"Maybe they're on break?"

Which was a possibility but, in Batya's eyes, a bit of a flimsy one. She'd been around way too many events to think

51

this was just a break. And just as she was about to say something, her phone started to buzz in her hand. Dr. Engleman was also reaching into his pocket.

For her, it was an email. On a blast to anybody who'd gotten involved with the competition.

George Gold drops out of the Rivertown latke competition

"Ill health," Dr. Engleman said, looking up at her.

"Way too many commitments," she said. She knew how it went. George had a big heart and worked with a bunch of different organizations. Rest and relaxation seemed like something that he had to be forced into.

"You know," Dr. Engleman said, "they're holding auditions for a host. It would seem rather convenient that someone who hosts a very interesting and relevant food-related website is in town."

"I couldn't," she said. "I really couldn't."

"And why not?"

There were many reasons she couldn't. "Doing interviews in an environment I control is much different than being up on stage during a competition where anything could go wrong," was the easiest, shortest way to say it. "You of all people should know that."

"I don't know that," he said. "I've seen you do this, Batya. You have time to practice before the auditions."

She smiled. "I appreciate your faith in me, but this isn't

something I can do."

Dr Engleman nodded, and she knew he was going to drop the subject.

But she still couldn't stop thinking about it.

>>><<<

DINNER WAS STILL at Sapna and Leo's, and Abe had once again arrived early.

"Set the table," Leo said as he went back to rejoin his wife and their daughter. "Nic's having a tantrum, and you don't want to be there."

"Noted," Abe said as his friend headed back to his daughter's room.

As he opened drawers, folding napkins and pulling out silverware, he started to think about recipes. Flour and apples and…

The loud bang on the front door yanked him right out of his reverie. Thankfully, it was Artur.

"You're early?" Abe asked.

Artur nodded, the wine and his choice of dessert settled in his arms. "I come early bearing usual sort of presents."

He raised an eyebrow. Artur's accent only showed up when he was exhausted, stressed, or drunk. "What's wrong?" he asked, banking on the former two.

"Not for me," he said as he walked toward the kitchen. "For you."

With Artur, there were always questions, interesting turns of phrase, and confusion. Which meant sometimes Abe had to push to get an answer that made sense. "What do you mean, exactly, by 'for me'?"

"There is," his friend finally said as he opened the fridge and removed a bottle of water, "something you need to know."

"What?"

"George Gold isn't hosting," he said. "Which means they're going to have tryouts for the host."

"How did you know?" Leo wondered, attempting to pick his jaw up off the floor. "You're not involved in the competition."

But Abe knew better and raised an eyebrow at Leo; Artur was, and had always been, a bottomless pit of information. People told Artur things, which was part of the reason why he was so good at his job. But more importantly, was it still worth it to stay in the competition?

"Meal Network will still film," Artur interjected, "there will still be a prize, and Gold will still mentor the winner and also whoever hosts."

"And no," Leo added, "you will not leave the competition and will not audition to host. You're too good a cook to sit on the sidelines."

Surprised once again by how well his friends knew him, Abe took a macaroon from one of the two bags Artur had left on the counter. "Okay. Fine. I'll stay in the competition as a contestant, and won't offer to try out and host. I will continue to prepare to make three nights' worth of latkes, and make all of you taste-test."

"Yes," Leo said as he swiped a soofganiyah from the second bag. "Good choice. And you'll win the competition. Keep us posted."

And as preparation for dinner began, he started to think about his flavors again. This would work.

He would win.

TUESDAY NIGHT WAS girl's night, and Batya was going to show her Hollowville friends that she wasn't leaving permanently by continuing the tradition. Even though Hollowville was only two miles on Route 9 away, and it never took long to find a parking space near Tante Shelly's apartment building, it felt like she'd gone much further.

Part of the reason was that she was going through Hollowville's bright downtown business district. The holiday lights were up, and the restaurants were flourishing in ways she hadn't appreciated before she went back to Rivertown. The stark contrast between the two towns made it more important that she tell her friends about what was happening just two miles away.

"I can't believe it," Anna said after Batya had told her friends the whole story.

"It's especially weird because the restaurants in Hollowville are booming," Sarah added. "New restaurants are opening—heck, even the stalwarts are expanding."

According to the rumor mill, even Chana was making noises about expansion, possibly into a second restaurant that would serve kosher meat.

"I think they're using the competition to try and catalyze a similar boom in Rivertown," Batya said. "Only they can't do it without a host."

"I thought George Gold was hosting—wasn't that the reason you agreed to go back there in the first place?" Anna noted.

Batya shook her head. "No. He pulled out this morning. But the competition is still being televised."

"So when are you going to apply?"

Batya blinked. "To what?"

Sarah sighed. "To host, that's what."

Which was, Batya noted, the second time someone she trusted had told her to apply. Which meant it was time to explain the problem. "I have stage fright," she admitted. "I can't do it. There are tryouts, and I will fail miserably."

"And what about your interviews?" Anna asked. "How do you do those?"

Even Batya had to admit her friend asked a really good question. "I think," she said after chewing on it for a second, "my problem is that after an incident that happened in high school, I haven't been able to deal with performance environments I don't control. I get horrible panic attacks. I set up my own environment for my interviews; I control pretty much every single aspect of things."

"What kind of things help you control the environment?" Sarah asked. "Memorized speeches? Friends in the audience? A particular outfit or scent in the room?"

"A little of all of them, I guess." Batya sighed.

"But what I want to know," Anna interjected as she took a sip of her tea, "is why. Like why do you do these interviews? Why do you organize all of this?"

Batya raised an eyebrow. "What do you mean?"

Anna shrugged. "As far as I know, you're going back to somewhere you practically swore you'd never see the inside of again, just because you want to do a website for a food competition and house-sit for your parents? I don't believe it. There's got to be more to it than that."

Sarah nodded. "I don't buy it either. I adore you. You know that. But you've seen both of us at our worst, our moments where we were at our lowest, and you helped us achieve what we were striving for. So, what's going on? Tell us."

Anna and Sarah were both right. She'd known them only for a short time, approaching six years now, but they'd bonded fast. They deserved to know her secret dream. "I've always wanted to do a show."

"What kind of show?" Sarah asked, her interest clearly piqued.

Which meant there was no stopping this; Sarah's fascination was like the tide. Batya sat back in her chair and took a long swallow of her tea. "It's been interesting over the past few years, and that's why I started the blog, the website, whatever you want to call FoodWorld. But I want to make it bigger. I want to tell stories."

"On walls? On paper?" Anna prompted.

Now she was in trouble. She had to admit the full story. "I want to tell stories about Jewish food on television. Especially on Meal Network."

Sarah made a noise Batya couldn't decipher.

"Interesting," Anna said as Sarah pulled herself together. "And what, pray tell, would doing a show on television require for you?"

And that was the rub, wasn't it? "Overcoming my stage fright."

"So," Sarah said with a smile, "I know the perfect way to start. Small. There's a little competition taking place in the next town over from here…"

And there was no denying that it was time for Batya to confront her fears, and start reaching for her dreams.

She could do this. She needed to try.

"Fine," she said. "I'll audition."

Anna nodded. "Good. Glad to hear."

"So," Sarah asked, "what can we do to help you prepare?"

Which was both the last thing she expected and the most predictable thing ever. And yet, she welcomed it all the same.

WHEN ABE GOT home from dinner, he checked his email only to find one from Dr. Engleman.

To: ANewman@LiebWaxmanTax.com
From: Englman@family.com

Dear Abe,

I'm writing to you, asking a favor.

I might need some help during the auditions this week. I wondered if you would volunteer to usher candidates.

You'll be one of several people doing this service.

I've attached a packet with the guidelines of what we're looking for here. Basically, you'll be responsible for helping them through the audition process itself, ferrying them to and from the ready room, which is my old classroom at Rivertown High School.

I know it's a big ask, because you've signed up to compete, but most people feel very much at ease around you.

Thank you in advance,
Dr. Engleman

Abe blew out a breath. There were very few people in this world, aside from his father, who thankfully was away on his cruise, who could ask him a question like this.

Of course he'd help.

Chapter Seven

B ATYA PREPARED FOR the audition as best she could, in the very same way she did her interviews. Research, note taking, minutes in front of her computer's camera.

But this wouldn't be an interview or even a situation she had control over.

It became more obvious, as she pulled into the RHS parking lot for the first time in more than ten years that she wasn't ready. Her hands were slick against the steering wheel; she could even feel the chills at the spot at the back of her neck that never symbolized anything good.

And every single quiz bowl mistake she'd ever made chose to run through her brain in a highlight reel of disaster. Every single mistake she'd made in a speech followed in quick succession.

Batya had to face facts; she wasn't cut out for television, or the stage, or the unpredictability of appearing in front of people and conveying anything but abject terror.

She tried to calm her breathing, to yank her head out of the spiral it had gone into.

She couldn't do this.

No matter how much she wanted it, no matter how desperately she wanted to take this step, a television show was way out of her league.

Which meant it was probably better for her to just go back to her parents' house and the safety of building the website.

Right?

As painful as this truth was to face, she should stop trying to dream, stop fantasizing.

Someone more charismatic, more exciting, more capable of driving and attracting the large audience the town needed, should be the host of the fry-off.

And if she repeated that conclusion often enough, she might make herself believe it.

She put her key back in the ignition and prepared to start her car again.

Someone knocked on the window.

She turned toward the sound, only to see…

Sarah?

Sarah Goldman, her friend Sarah, the Sarah who was about to be named chair of the Hollowville Hanukkah Festival committee, was standing outside the car, in Rivertown, waving and smiling at her.

Holy crap.

"What are you doing?" Batya asked as she got out of the car. "Aren't you busy? Why are you…?"

"Clearly," her friend said with a smile, "because you were

literally about to leave, you absolutely needed us."

"I didn't expect you'd come."

"Yeah," Sarah continued, smiling as Isaac, of all people, handed her a rather large, slightly chilled paper cup. "But we're here anyway."

Batya gratefully took the cup from Isaac's outstretched hands, noting the long straw that stuck out from the top. "What is this?"

"This is tea," Sarah explained. "Chana's special mint tea. Your favorite."

It was.

But Sarah was busy with the beginning of preparations for the Hanukkah festival, and the things she had to do before it turned the life of the presumptive festival chair into chaos. "You two drove here with this for me?"

"She didn't drive," Anna said, grinning as she joined them.

"You're kidding," Batya said in disbelief. Sarah, Isaac, and Anna had shown up.

"Not kidding," Sarah replied.

"So who drove? Because clearly someone did."

"Jacob's looking for parking," Anna said. "He was too stubborn to take my car with the sticker, and so he's looking for parking."

They were all here. Even as Jacob joined the group, his arrival heralding more jokes about his insistence on paying for parking, Batya felt…she didn't know what to feel. Loved was close. Embraced was better.

"You're here," she managed, the words keeping her anchored to the scene. "You're here."

"We're not that far away," Sarah pointed out. "We're in Hollowville, and you are nervous. And you don't think I was listening when you said friends in the audience might help you be less nervous?"

"She reorganized her schedule for this," Isaac pointed out. "Chana is running the meeting."

"You missed a meeting for me," Batya said as the air started to flow back into her lungs, the magnitude of what her friend had done shoving the fear away. "I—"

"Oh my God," Sarah said as Jacob took the cup away and she and Anna put their arms around Batya. "You're going to do great. Now come on." Sarah stepped back. "Where do we have to go?"

With Sarah, Isaac, Anna, and Jacob by her side, Batya was ready to head into the audition. She opened the door, and it felt as if no time had passed. The high school even smelled the same.

But as if Sarah realized the awkwardness of the moment, she said, "I am so tempted to sing the Hollowville school song right now."

"Please don't," Isaac said as he put his arm around Sarah. "I don't think we had a school song."

"You went to private school," Sarah pointed out as she leaned into the embrace. "They don't."

Jacob shook his head. "We did, but this Westchester rivalry stuff is beyond me."

"You went to public school," Anna pointed out. "I'd guess Long Island is the same or worse. All the same, if only to save my ears from that wretched piece of ridiculousness, please don't sing it, Sarah."

"I don't even remember the Rivertown school song," Batya admitted.

"Conveniently," yet another voice added, "it's on that banner right there. And I can help you remember."

Jacob had given her back the tea, but the shock of Abe's random interjection into the conversation made her send it flying everywhere.

It was iced, thankfully, but still.

Her jacket was covered. Sarah looked at Isaac, who snorted as she grabbed the jacket.

Anna reached into her purse and pulled out a bleach stick. "Here," she said and passed the stick to Sarah.

"Why are you here?" Batya asked Abe as her friends tried to deal with the jacket. "What exactly are you trying to do?"

Abe, that handsome, annoying fakakta schmuck, shook his head, then ran a hand through his curly dark blond hair and sighed. "Nothing," he said. "Dr. Engleman asked me to help out today, bring audition candidates to the ready room." He paused. "And I guess that includes you?"

"Oh really. Freaking misguided yentas everywhere trying to remind me of my worst mistake."

"Not yours," he said. "My mistake."

"Can you just stop it? This is the worst remake of a teen movie I have ever been in, and I would rather not continue to be the star, 'kay?"

And then Batya realized what she'd said and in front of whom. Her Hollowville friends were just standing there. As if any of them had ever, or would ever, pass up the opportunity to comment on a situation like this.

"Abe," she said grudgingly. This was definitely her worst nightmare. "This is Sarah, Isaac, Anna, and Jacob. They're from Hollowville. Guys, this is Abe Newman, from Rivertown. We went to high school together."

Batya tried to ignore the undertone and the sharp hiss as Anna elbowed Jacob into silence. She'd simplified the situation, and if Jacob or Isaac had issues with being characterized as being from Hollowville, they had bigger problems than she could fix.

"It's nice to meet all of you," Abe said before turning to her. "I'm sorry. Dr. Engleman is using his old room for the ready room, so in your case, I'll make an exception. I'll show your friends where the auditorium is, then I'll meet you at his room when it's time to bring you over. Just tell him for me."

"You're already having me make excuses for you?"

"There is no excuse for me," he quipped.

The professional she was did not laugh, but she did nod. "See you guys after?"

There were nods, hugs, hopes for broken legs and a joke about broken microphones.

Finally, after Batya soaked up the last bit of all of that excited, loving energy, she headed down the hallway, nervous that despite all of the work she'd put in, this was going to end horribly.

ABE HAD NEVER before been in front of an audience this hostile. Maybe once. But not like this.

"Look," he said. "Just treat me like an usher."

"This group," the tall thin guy with shoulders bigger than he'd ever seen said, "thinks spilling tea is flirting."

"She spilled it on herself, not on him. Now if she'd spilled it on him," the gal with the curly brown hair said, "it would be a different story. He deserves the dry cleaning bill."

"Make him pay for the dry cleaning," the gal with the straight brown hair said. "Only decent thing to do."

"The last thing," the other guy, the one who'd been elbowed by the gal with the straight hair, said with the slightest Long Island accent, "Batya would probably want is for this guy to have access to her clothing without her knowing. He should *offer* to pay for the dry cleaning, with a text or an email."

And then a pause, and Abe found himself meeting this man's blue eyes. This one could easily eat them all for breakfast.

"Not just offer but insist. And maybe apologize for stepping over boundaries she wanted kept in the process."

"Not everybody can get away with *insisting* on paying for someone's dry cleaning," the other guy said, "but it is a good idea, Jacob. You should absolutely give it a shot."

Abe nodded. "I'll see what I can do. But if I don't get your group into the auditorium, we're all going to be in trouble."

Which was an extremely scary thought. Facing Batya's wrath, or Dr. Engleman's, wasn't exactly the way he wanted to start the day. Or end it, as the case may be.

»»»«««

IT FELT IMPOSSIBLY strange to be walking through the hallways of Rivertown High School for the first time since she'd graduated. The place even smelled the same, which was weird. Because clearly Rivertown High was not preserved as a cautionary exhibit for future high school students.

No. Not totally cautionary.

The quiz bowl community had embraced her when she transferred from Shechter in the ninth grade, the one awkward Jewish day school girl joining the freshman class along with a wave of former Catholic school kids. In quiz bowl Batya found her crowd and a teacher she could trust to explain things she'd missed.

"Oh, I'm so glad to see you decided to audition," Dr. Engleman said as she walked into the room. "I think you'll do a great job," he said, smiling.

"I appreciate your faith in me," she said, "but I have to tell you that being in this room, in this place, feels strange."

"Time capsule? It's funny, how easy it was to come back to this place. I've been retired now for quite a few years and being here feels like nothing has changed."

She sighed. "You'd think it was senior year and the AP exam was a month away."

"Flashbacks even I would rather not have," Dr. Engleman said with a laugh.

And as she chatted to her favorite teacher, Batya's shoulders loosened; her hands stopped sweating.

She could breathe.

"I can do this," Batya said in an attempt to convince Dr. Engleman as well as herself.

I can do this.

Just like she'd done any interview on and for her website.

"Hey."

The voice was familiar. Abe.

"They're ready for her?" Dr Engleman asked.

Abe nodded. "They are." And then he turned to her. "You ready?"

She didn't joke or laugh or smile. This wasn't funny; this was serious. "Yes," she said. "I am."

And without any fanfare, he led her down the hall, down

passages she'd taken so many times she could follow them with her eyes closed.

"They're settled in the auditorium," he said. "I mean the Hollowville peeps who came to see you."

She nodded. "Thanks."

"Is it better if I don't talk?"

She started to feel tightness in her shoulders, and there was only one thing that fixed that problem. Which meant she was about to make a horrible mistake. "Can I ask you a weird favor?"

He raised an eyebrow. "Sure. Whatever."

"Can you...can you give me a shoulder massage?"

He paused, and she wasn't sure what he was thinking— maybe of the moments in the green room before a quiz bowl match. Maybe of the moments where he was the one who lifted the entire team's spirits in any way he could.

And asking him for a massage was the worst possible thing she could do but she was desperate and she needed it.

Instead of answering or making some weird quip, he cracked his knuckles, the sound echoing across the hall. And then he placed his hands on her shoulders. She felt the motion on her shoulder blades, on the muscles that seemed to almost lock her shoulders in position. His fingers seemed to find the tightest part of her muscles and through motion and magic, loosened them.

"Tell me if this is too hard."

"It's fine," she managed as the touch of his hands sent

her into a state of boneless happiness, way beyond simple relaxation.

"You good?"

She nodded. She could do this.

"All right then," he said. "Here we go."

But as she stepped through the double doors that separated the backstage area from the stage itself, her heart started to pound and the sweat began to pour down the back of her neck.

Breathe.

Her hands started to shake. She grabbed on to her phone in her pocket. She could hold that. Couldn't she?

She needed to hold something.

And then her shirt, the gorgeous turtleneck sweater she'd chosen, was getting too tight around her neck. She shoved the phone back into her pocket and started to pull at the collar of the sweater. Oh God. Not now, not again.

"Batya?"

Abe's voice sounded calm, but she could see he wasn't.

She was going to fail. Horribly.

In front of everybody. In front of Sarah who'd missed a meeting, Anna who'd stopped doing *something*, and everybody else who'd fought traffic to be here.

They had faith in her, all of them.

Even Abe.

She tried to find words in the depths of her throat. "Hi…"

"Batya."

Abe's voice wrapped around her like a fuzzy blanket, and she grabbed on to it with both hands. She focused on the sound and the warmth in his tones.

"You can do this," he said. "I believe in you. I see you."

And then she could feel him taking her hand in his. She took a deep breath, focusing on the feel of his hand. The weight of it, the heat of it against hers.

"You with me?"

She nodded. It was hard, so freaking hard, but she did it. "I'm here."

He nodded. "I'm here as long as you need me."

And if nothing else, that gave her the space to focus on what was happening, to breathe, to feel the touch and pull herself out of the spiral she'd gone down in. "I'm here," she said again. "I'm here."

"You ready?"

She nodded. And in a way, his presence made it easier for her to take the space she needed. She closed her eyes and let herself imagine what it would be like if things had been different, if he could be there supporting her for real, not just because he'd been assigned to. And as she pulled herself away from the fantasy, she could breathe. "Ready."

"What you're going to have to do is read the teleprompter as if you were on television. Okay?"

She bit her lip. "Okay."

It wasn't. It wouldn't be.

But she said it anyway.

"I'll stay until you can."

Which was not what she expected, but he was willing to stand with her, and if her ridiculous zombie crush was enough to overcome her stage fright for more than five minutes, she'd give it the victory.

If it could be called a victory when she stared up at the monitor and tried to breathe, read words with a voice that had forgotten language, her tongue tripping on everything as the room faded further and further away.

She blew out a breath. But when she opened her eyes to focus on the monitor again, the screen was blank.

Completely and utterly blank.

"Can you continue?" Kiyoshi. From the audience. "No prompter, so just continue."

Continue? How?

Batya immediately went into website mode. There were programs that turned browsers in to teleprompters these days. She could fix a website, she could fix this. "Is it a software problem or a hardware problem?"

Kiyoshi blinked. "What?"

Batya smiled, back in her element, the stage fright gone. "Teleprompters are weird things, and they could have trouble whether we're dealing with either a software or hardware issue."

"An audition issue."

"What?" she asked.

"Tech can go wrong," he said wryly, "so we're judging how everybody can host if there's a problem. Improvisation is important, you know."

Batya nodded, and for some reason she didn't feel the pressure in her chest anymore. "So, if this is a tech question, then the best thing…"

Wait.

She could take control of the situation.

"Give me a second."

She didn't even see Kiyoshi's response as she made a bee-line to the laptop on the table. She turned it on, typed a few keys, and presto, the projector showed her website and the background she'd made for Hanukkah the year before.

"Tonight is a special night," she began, reading the introduction she'd written last night, typed up, and animated, "where we're making one of our most famous celebratory foods. They're fun, fungible, and a wonderful crunchy bit of our history. We eat latkes to celebrate, we eat latkes to enjoy, but tonight we begin the journey of using latkes to learn about the restaurant community in Rivertown. The restaurants that have contributed ingredients to the competition are strong partners in Rivertown's growth, and it is our hope that the winner of the competition finds strong and special roots here in Rivertown for years to come." She grinned. "Are we ready to get started?"

There was a pause, and she knew there would be.

A member of the committee, someone she didn't know,

meandered their way up onto the stage with a bag and an index card.

"Okay, everybody," Batya said as she took the card out. "Tonight's bag comes from a restaurant we all love. Fratelli's restaurant is owned by a second-generation Rivertown resident, but it was started by a restaurateur who began his career and his life in Italy." She trailed off, hearing the cheers from the audience, possibly from Leo?

Who was standing in the middle of the audience with the entire rest of her quiz bowl team and her Hollowville friends.

And Abe, just off to the side, standing between the backstage area and the door.

Which was also beyond her capacity for thought.

"I think," Kiyoshi said with a smile, "you've done what we asked. Thank you, Batya."

As she left the auditorium, and the scenario played through her mind, she realized that she wasn't exactly sure how she'd managed to get through the audition. But she had. And now she might actually have a chance to get the hosting job. Maybe.

No matter what, she still had the website. And her friends, who despite everything, had come to support her.

And if she told herself that enough times, she'd start to believe it.

Chapter Eight

B ATYA OPENED HER email the next morning, prepared to
deal with some administrative details she'd been
ignoring. But there were two emails that grabbed her attention immediately.

The first was from Abe.

To: BAverman@foodworld.com
From: ANewman@LiebWaxmanTax.com

I hope you're doing better this morning.

    **For what it's worth, and I have absolutely no in-
put in any decision they make, I think you did a
pretty good job.**

    **But I still feel horrible about the tea stains. As a
way of giving you a more tangible apology, I'd like to
pay for your dry cleaning. Please send me the bill at
this address. It's the least I can do.**

Abe

She had no idea how to respond to that, and so read the
email from Kiyoshi marked Important Business instead.

To: BAverman@foodworld.com

From: KTakayama@Rivertown.NY.gov

Batya,

The committee enjoyed your audition, but they're looking for something that demonstrates the influence you have in the food community.

What would you say to teaching a class to the participants of the fry-off over the span of, say five weeks, with the objective of bringing traffic to your website as well as the website for the fry-off, with guest lecturers drawn from your contacts?

Let me know.

Kiyoshi

Because both of those emails were going to require thoughtful answers, Batya went to the kitchen and made herself a cup of tea and an omelet.

The hot drink and the sizzling sound of the oil made her relax, and the focus on the egg mixture took her concentration, forcing her to think about her end goals.

Did she want to teach a class, with the help of guests, for the participants?

Did she want to teach about Jewish foodways and the things that made Jewish-American food special?

Of course she did. Having guest lecturers would absolutely help her present the material, and the organization of the class would help her deal with her stage fright. It was a complete fluke that she was able to take advantage of a *tech* issue to calm her sweaty palms and pounding heart in the middle of the audition.

But who could she ask? Who did she want to ask?

She sat down, took out a pen, and wrote a list, in the very same way she'd always advised her friends when they had to make important decisions.

After a few minutes, she turned on the most recent Shadow Squad movie (for background noise, of course) and tried to think about how she could execute the vision she had for the class. And who could help make that vision a reality.

Charlotte? Could Charlotte come in to talk about what many people got wrong about challah?

Anna? For sure. Anna could talk about the history of Jewish foodways and spices, especially the demonization of Ashkenazi food.

Who else? Who else could she ask?

Chana could talk about the specifics of cooking dairy.

She had an interview with Abraham Kaplan, the owner of Abe's Kitchen scheduled for the website. Could she ask him to talk to the group about Jewish meat, the way he saw Jewish-American food, and why his deli was so important?

Yes. All of them. And if they said no, she could maybe ask other people, take the class in different directions. But this would work for now. And she wrote up a proposal, just like she would if she was approaching any other client.

To: KTakayama@Rivertown.NY.gov
From: BAverman@foodworld.com

Kiyoshi,

Here's the proposal for the class. Subject to change based on availability of the instructors, but these are my ideas.
Let me know.

B

She left the email window open but headed into the program she was using to design the fry-off's website, checked code, and then went back into the notes she'd made. She wanted to focus on the work she was supposed to do instead of the email she was waiting for.

She also realized she was hungry, and the omelet was long done, so she got up and grabbed some mango slices before sitting back down.

Beep. Her email program. Her hands were sweating as she read Kiyoshi's message.

To: BAverman @foodworld.com
From: KTakayama@Rivertown.NY.gov

B,

Charlotte Liu for challah? Really?
I mean I love it, but...why?

K

She'd expected questions, but for some dumb reason, not that one. People who made arbitrary decisions about who could cook Jewish food bothered her immensely, and for some reason it bothered her more that he was one of them.

Probably because she hadn't expected him to be that

small-minded.

She tried not to be too angry, because she couldn't yell at him in person and this was going into an email, which meant there would be documentation. She cracked her knuckles.

To: KTakayama
From: BAverman

Because she makes some of the best challah I've ever tasted and way too many non-Jews are like that British chef who says that braided bread is boring, and that all bread recipes, including challah, need butter. I also did her website, and she's friends with a friend of mine.

I notice you didn't ask me about any of the others.

This response was harder to wait for, so she took a few more mango slices from the container and chewed thoughtfully as she leaned against the unforgiving back of the kitchen chair. There were books all around her, cookbooks and books about the patterns of Jewish immigration and...

Beep.

Once again, she opened the window and braced herself for his response.

To: BAverman
From: KTakayama

True. I didn't ask you about Abe from Abe's Kitchen either, but I also would like to know what your con-

nection to him is, and how you'd get him to agree to guest lecture.

This was a better response than she'd expected; this from Kiyoshi was an acknowledgment. He was now framing it about credentials and her access, which she was glad to talk about.

To: KTakayama
From: BAverman

I have an interview with him scheduled, but I'll see if he's willing to do this instead. I said subject to availability.
    Did you read the website?

Ugh. This email was harder to wait for because poking her friend was different than poking her friend as a professional on his email. But it was necessary. She swallowed a huge gulp of tea before turning back to the website. And hoped for the better.

And then there was a beep.

To: BAverman
From: KTakayama

I didn't, but Abe did. He sings your praises. I like what you're designing for the fry-off website though.

What was their obsession with Abe Newman, or more specifically, shoving his name in her face?

Instead of even addressing that comment, she realized

she'd forgotten to put a name down on the proposed instructor list. Which gave her an easy way out and something important to type:

To: KTakayama
From: BAverman

I think the head of the Hollowville festival committee (pending a vote) could be convinced to come in and talk about Hanukkah traditions around the world and why this particular food tradition is fun and flexible and the best.

There. That should close the topic on Mr. Newman and get Kiyoshi thinking about more connections. And other things.

She took a few more mango slices and picked up the Melanie Gould book Sarah and Anna had given her. So far, the story of a banking heir falling in love with a dressmaker in the East End of London was more engrossing than she'd expected; she could see why someone like Sam Moskowitz would want to star in the adaptation even though it wasn't her usual fare. But she put the book down when she heard the beep of an incoming email.

To: BAverman
From: KTakayama

That sounds great. I'll send this over to the committee and let you know what they say.
I notice you didn't say anything about Abe singing your praises.

A relief and yet not at the same time. The last thing she wanted to do was tell Kiyoshi to stop trying to be a matchmaker in a professional email. But she had absolutely no choice.

To: KTakayama
From: BAverman

Stop. I don't need to remake the horrible nightmare that was my senior year, thank you. You graduated two years before so you didn't have to witness it. It's as bad as the stories say.

There. Hopefully, that would stop the problem, and she turned back to the book and her mango slices, until there was a beep.

Once again, it was from Kiyoshi, but this time it was from his personal address.

She shook her head and clicked on the email.

To: BAverman
From: KTakayama@friendmail.com (personal)

Your senior year was not a nightmare. One incident doesn't a nightmare make. I seem to remember some very good ones when I came back from college to watch the back end. And the quiz bowl victory at State.

Interesting. Very, very interesting. She had to call him on this.

To: KTakayama@friendmail.com
From: BAverman

Interesting. Switched emails. Why?

This time, she didn't click out of the program but instead waited for the response. What was he on about this time? And she got her answer as quickly as she'd sent one, apparently.

To: BAverman
From: KTakayama (personal)

The fewer references to your senior year on the professional email the better, especially when I'm telling you I remember them.
    Anyway. I'll send the proposal to the committee on the professional email and keep you posted.
    For what it's worth, I think they'll bite. I think this class will be good for them and good for you.
    And no matter what position you have for the competition, it's going to be good.
    I believe in you even if I can't say it.
    Abe does too. We all do.

K

Of course he had to stick in the last Abe reference.

But things were set. She was getting a chance at an extended audition for a hosting position she wanted with every fiber of her being.

Unfortunately, she was starting to realize that the more

time she spent in Rivertown, the more she and Abe were going to randomly rub up against each other. She'd see him in places everybody in town went—the farmers' market and Baum's already—they were already tied together by the persistent matchmakers from their quiz bowl class. And now they were also both involved in the competition; he'd be one of the people taking her class.

Not to mention how calming Abe had been and how willing he'd been to stick his neck out for her during the audition. It wasn't just the massage; it was the time, the focus. And the complete lack of judgment.

Which meant she had to do something about him, not just respond to the email he'd sent her this morning about dry cleaning bills.

But what exactly did she want to do?

If nothing else, she was going to find out why the heck he wanted to try to pay for her dry cleaning, and maybe somehow repay him for his kindness at the audition. And that meant doing something she'd never actually done.

Calling him on the phone.

When, of course, she'd psyched herself up to do it.

ABE WAS CUTTING vegetables, preparing for the weekend's barbecue, but he was also experimenting with applesauce. The apple slices were cooking on the stove with a few spices.

His phone rang.

"Hello?"

"Why is it so important that you pay for my dry cleaning?"

He had no idea Batya even had his number, and he wasn't sure exactly why she'd decided to call him, but he swallowed and pushed ahead. In for a penny, he guessed. "Because it's the right thing to do. I'm responsible for—"

"Nope. You are not responsible for this. There are things you're responsible for, Abe Newman, but the cost of cleaning my clothing is not one of them. Besides," she said, "you also went above and beyond last night, so I figure I owe you."

"You don't owe me," he replied almost instantly. "I didn't help you to even out some scale. I helped you because you needed it."

There was a long pause. Had he lost her, or was she thinking? He wished he could see her, tease out the expression in her eyes.

"Look," she said, "at our worst, which is often, we're a disaster made in some mad scientist's lab. We're a snowman and summer. We don't mix. But every time we're around each other, our mutual friends either want to shove us together or tiptoe around us, and I don't want that kind of energy all the time. It's exhausting, and I'm sick of it."

"So what do you want?" he asked because he couldn't think of any other response.

"I don't know. I don't want to force my friends to expend that much energy just because you and I are in the same room together. I want some kind of safe place, and I'm starting to think that isn't possible."

What she was really trying to say was that she wanted to cut ties instead of create them. Which made any words he could say dry up and shrivel inside of him.

But there was an obligation here, and he needed to take care of it. So whatever he offered had to be a joke. A pun.

And then he had it.

"How do you feel about ice cream?"

"I don't follow. I mean, I like ice cream. A lot. More than I should, frankly, but there you go."

"How about," he suggested, as if he weren't making a last-ditch effort at saving this phone call, "you let me buy you ice cream? It's cold outside, or will be."

"Why?"

He smiled. He could do this. "So that way, you can't say I didn't get you ice in winter."

She laughed.

The sound of her laugh made him warm inside, and dear God this was wonderful and dangerous all at the same time. It almost felt normal, which was something he'd never been able to manage with her. What was this alternate reality where dealing with a phone call from her made him calm down?

"Are you serious?"

Was that shock or sarcasm in her voice? He had no idea,

but he was going to be honest even if honest sounded ridiculous. "Yes," he said, leading with the easy part. "You have my word. Even better, you have all of them."

There was silence, and it wasn't the good kind. It was awkward, and made him feel like he'd gone from comfortable warmth into an icy bath. There were reasons he wasn't a fan of polar plunges no matter how many good causes the plunges were for.

Finally, she sighed, and the sound almost ripped his heart out.

He braced himself for the blow he knew was coming. He wasn't going to ask her what she'd take. But just as he was going to say something, she spoke.

"Fine," she said. "If you want to buy me ice cream, sure. But this means nothing other than you tried to pay for my dry cleaning."

Was she agreeing to this? Did he succeed in this wild, ridiculous, grabbing-at-straws sort of plan?

But he couldn't seem too joyful about the whole thing. He had to act as nonchalant as possible, otherwise he'd scare the crap out of her. "I get it. It doesn't mean anything other than ice cream. You don't even have to sit with me."

"But what if I want to?"

Wait…what? But once again, he couldn't let his surprise show. "Fair," he said.

"As long as we're talking fair, how about I buy you ice cream first? Like, I'll pay the first time, and maybe you send me ice cream afterward?"

Ah, she didn't want to feel obligated. "That," he said, "sounds like a plan."

"Do you want to meet at Rivertown Ice at three?"

"That works."

And when he hung up the phone, he was cautiously optimistic.

Way too early to admit he was excited.

Way too early.

RIVERTOWN ICE.

Same location. Still serving all things frozen. But all the sameness belied the change that had taken place. Three different ownership groups, including the ill-fated attempt at a crepe shop her mother still yelled about from time to time.

But the sign above the door looked as if nothing had changed. It reminded Batya of high school traditions and quiz bowl celebrations. Even the menu looked as if it had been pulled directly from her memory.

"New owners are descended from the original ones," Abe said. "They're trying to bring the place back to the way it was."

"I can see that," she said.

"How does it feel?"

"Like everything and nothing has changed at the same

time." And that felt more like a thing George Gold would say on one of his shows.

But Abe didn't call her out on it. Food history was their common ground, it seemed. They could *talk* about and around food. And, God, that was what she wanted, staring at the excitement in his eyes, feeling her heart pound.

More than that was dangerous.

Wanting more than that was dangerous.

Admitting she wanted more than that was dangerous.

"Makes sense," he said, yanking her back to reality and gesturing to the crew behind the counter. "Grandchildren. Wanting to hold on to the memory and the space their grandfather made for the town. And, of course"—he gestured toward the dairy-free, sugar-free and low-sugar section—"make this a place where everybody can eat."

"And remember," she replied with a grin, "this is on me."

They headed to the counter and took their ice cream samplers to a table in the back corner of the restaurant, where they could see the back garden covered in leaves and dressed for fall.

"This is nice," she said. "I like it."

"Ice cream is a universal solvent," he said with a laugh.

"This doesn't say anything but thank you for being there for me when I was having that panic attack," she replied.

He nodded. "I know. Just…it's nice to hang out with you."

Hang out with you.

No. No. No.

She focused on the ice cream. "You can actually taste the flavors here," she said. "I really like them."

"Which one's your favorite?"

She pondered for a few minutes before she answered. "Rum raisin is always my favorite, but this version makes me very happy. I love the cookie dough too. And the birthday cake."

"They're really good with that vanilla base of theirs. I love a bunch of their other flavors. They're having a lot of fun too."

And if Batya was going to be honest with herself, so was she. Talking to Abe was easy as long as she was able to talk about food. The excitement about spending time with him carried her home, and as she sat down to work on the website, her phone buzzed.

An email. Her first thought was that it was from Abe, and she wasn't prepared for the letdown when she saw it wasn't.

Danger, danger, Batya Averman.

It was from Kiyoshi.

The council had accepted her proposal, and all she had to do was organize the guest instructors and the schedule.

Holy crap.

Now the question was whether she could do it. She also had a contract for the website, and as she stuck the adorable latke emoji she'd drawn on the top right corner of the front page, she had to admire it; it was the beginning of something special for her hometown, something they'd pass from generation to generation, like Hollowville passed down the Hanukkah festival.

It felt good. There was nothing in the world that could make her mood any better.

Until she sat back against the chair, and the phone buzzed against the kitchen table again.

>>>><<<<

ABE WAS ANNOYED. Not because he'd had a bad time—far from it. But this moment of truce had happened without him even broaching the subject of the dry cleaning and his part of the ice cream debt.

And that meant he had to call her. He checked his shopping list first, of course, to make sure he didn't seem too eager, too interested in keeping contact. Finally, when it felt like enough time had passed, he called her.

"Hey," he said as she picked up the phone. "It was good to see you today."

"I had a good time too."

"Listen," he said.

"Wait. I need to tell you something."

"What?" And then he paused, checked his email. "You're going to do a class starting Wednesday?"

"Yeah. I am. How did you find out?"

"Just got the email." He paused. "I'm a competitor, so..."

"Right. So what is it you want to say?"

"There's something we didn't talk about."

"Please. I'm not ready to talk about graduation."

"Not what I meant. I still need to send you ice cream."

"Why, exactly? We had ice cream; life is groovy. We're good."

"Because," he said, sighing. "I told you I'd send you ice cream. You know, for the dry cleaning. But also, you were stressed as it was, so the last thing you needed was to worry about tea spilled on your clothing."

She didn't say anything in response, not instantly, so he took that as a victory. "I need your address."

He didn't think she was going to answer. He was convinced she was going to tell him she'd made a mistake and couldn't accept anything from him for any number of reasons. He was prepared for that; this was, after all, how his relationship with Batya had gone up till this point.

The pause, however, was almost comfortable. Almost.

"If you're still insistent about it, I'm staying at my parents' house," she finally said in a way that sounded like she was surprising even herself. "I'll give you the address."

And that felt like a victory, one he was more than willing to take.

Chapter Nine

BATYA FOUND THAT it was much easier to talk about the class and do the research for it, than manage the nerves that filled her on Wednesday, the day she was going to start teaching it. She'd done the prep work, of course. Checked her notes, confirmed Charlotte and Tony were going to get to Rivertown at around 6:15 so they could go over the lecture and the format it would take. By 5:30 she'd swallowed some chicken broth and some matzah balls, settling her stomach as best she could, before she drove over to the high school.

But despite all of that prep work, her hands were still shaking as she headed into the auditorium. Breathing was an impossibility.

She could do this, she reminded herself. She could really do this.

And if she said it enough, she'd start to believe it.

"Batya?"

She lifted her head to see Charlotte step into the room, her husband Tony close behind.

"Hi," she answered. "I'm here. Thank you for…for coming…"

Through the fog, Batya could see her friend put down her tote and head toward her. Charlotte veered behind her, pressing experienced fingers on her shoulders. Massaging shoulders and kneading dough were apparently the same thing.

"You're going to be fine," Charlotte said as she finished rubbing and came around. "I can do a lot of the heavy lifting if you need me to."

Batya shook her head despite the rising panic, the nerves. "No. It's fine. I just have to get through this be-cause…because…" She forced herself to breathe and slow down. "Because otherwise what's the point of even doing this at all?"

Charlotte nodded. "Fair enough. These classes are im-portant. And you have my help when you need it."

And as Batya started to actually calm down, she saw Abe come through the entrance. He didn't stop by, didn't say hello, but she watched him head up the stairs, straight for a seat. And when he settled down…that's when he smiled, looking directly at her.

If nothing else, she'd manage this class, focusing on his smile.

ON WEDNESDAY NIGHT, the night of the first class, Abe

found a seat toward the back, on the far side, a few seats away from the aisle.

There was a whiteboard at the center of the front of the auditorium, and he could hear Batya chatting with someone off to the side. He wasn't going to bother her; he wasn't there to make jokes. He was there to learn, and be a friendly face in the crowd. But when he settled into his seat, he caught her eye and smiled.

When she smiled back, he could breathe just a little bit.

Finally, it was 7:00.

"Hello, everybody," Batya began as she came to the front of the room. He could see how nervous she was, tight words pushed out between her teeth, the way her hands grabbed on to the chair she was going to sit on.

"Welcome to the class."

She stopped, and he wanted to get up and run down the aisle to help her. But at the same time, he knew that the best way of being supportive was to let her do this. To be there if she needed him, if she wanted him—but she had to teach the class on her own.

"My name is Batya Averman," she continued. "This will be our introduction to Jewish foodways, and will serve as a five-week prelude to the fry-off you have all registered for."

There was going to be a joke. He could feel it, and he would not let it fall flat no matter what state she delivered it in.

And sure enough, a small, wry smile appeared on her

face. "Last chance to leave for anything easier or more interesting."

Which wasn't a joke, but he smiled and gave a tiny finger clap. Her headshake was a victory.

"Just a reminder," she said, grasping the lectern in a way he was sure made her knuckles white, "this class is streaming, so hello to everybody at home."

And because he couldn't resist, he yelled, "Hello, everybody!" before turning to wave at the camera at the back of the room.

Thankfully, the rest of the class joined him.

And even though she seemed a little annoyed, he could see the slight drop of her shoulders, a tell-tale sign she was also relaxing.

"The class will also be available for viewing on my website, foodworld.com, as well as Rivertownfry-off.com. Tonight's lecture will also be available on Cs-place.com."

And then there was a long pause as the class got themselves together for the announcement of the lecturer. He knew who it was going to be, of course, but the rest of the class had to wait in suspense.

"Tonight's lecturer is a brilliant chef, restauranteur, and baker. She's here from Rockliffe Manor, but she has restaurants in both Manhattan and in Brooklyn, as well as the restaurant and pastry shop in Rockliffe Manor. She's here to talk about one of the most fundamentally Jewish foods."

He held his breath as she paused, watching her hands

open and close, her fingers pressing and releasing on her palms.

He tried to catch her gaze.

Breathe in, breathe out.

A slightly shaky nod before she went back to her notes.

Victory.

"We eat it all the time, on Friday nights, on Saturday mornings, and every single day in between. Breakfast specialties, sandwiches at lunch. It can be anything and do anything. I'm talking about challah."

There was excitement in the room, and he couldn't wait.

"May I introduce you all to my friend, Charlotte Liu."

He'd seen Charlotte on TV, but up close was different. She was mesmerizing. But not as mesmerizing as Batya.

The chef had a cooler over her shoulder, and a guy who seemed familiar trailed behind her.

Who was he?

And then he remembered.

Tony Liu was an accountant and financial manager who used to work at one of the other firms. From what Abe knew, Tony had left that firm three years before and now was in private practice in Rockliffe Manor.

He also remembered seeing Tony's name on some of the tax documents he'd worked with for his independent republic client. But Abe wasn't here to collect gossip about accountants; he was here to learn from Charlotte about challah.

And she knew her stuff, clearly. The woman spoke about parve cooking and why it was important that a bread like challah was parve and versatile.

"So," Batya said, looking a bit more comfortable as she was able to let Charlotte take the spotlight, "it is not best with butter?"

"Only a fool would say that," Charlotte replied with a laugh. "Same fool who would say that nobody braids anything anymore. This is tradition, and if I get it, everybody should."

Abe laughed along with the rest of the class. There were a lot of notes taken. Tony passed along the cooler containing the bread in stages, giving Abe a nod in the process. Which was interesting.

And so was the class, especially when Charlotte, Tony, and Batya handed out slices of freshly baked challah.

Batya gave him his and smiled, which he was grateful for, but he wasn't quite sure she was. He didn't know that smile.

But as everybody, including him, was eating every single crumb of their slice, they settled down to listen to the last question of the class.

"What lesson do you want to pass along to everybody today?" Batya asked Charlotte. "What's the one thing you want everybody to know?"

"People need to know the history of food before they start working with it," Charlotte replied. "Challah is history. Challah is tradition. You can't work with it, you can't attempt to 'improve' it, without understanding where it came from and why it is the way it is. Can you change tradition? Yes. But only when you know where it's been."

"Which," Batya said, "leads into next week's class, where we'll learn about Jewish-American foodways and our traditions."

And he couldn't wait to get started, and make a challah of his own.

THE NEXT DAY, while Batya was making notes and watching a George Gold marathon on the Meal Network, there was a knock on the door.

A delivery today?

She was fairly sure she hadn't ordered anything after her decadent dinner with Charlotte and Tony. But the delivery guy carried a special cooler.

"Delivery from Rivertown Ice."

Ice cream?

She took the box inside, deciding it would be safer to open it on the kitchen table, unearthing the cool packs and a card.

Instead of diving into the flavor he'd sent her, she decided to behave like an adult and open the card first.

Dear Batya,

Raisins are controversial in challah. I like them myself,

but I don't put them in ones I've attempted to make because not everybody has the affinity I do.

But you said that this was your favorite when we came here this past week. So here it is.

Happy eating,
Abe

All she could do was savor the rum raisin ice cream he sent her, and remember how much she'd enjoyed the sampler.

She'd figure out how to thank him later.

If he managed to keep this up.

ON FRIDAY AFTERNOON, Abe was relaxing, enjoying himself as he started to prepare the things he needed for tomorrow's setup. Sauce first. Bowls and ingredients were strewn out across the table, and the music he played was the perfect soundtrack for the moment.

Thankfully, he hadn't put it up too loud, because there was a knock at the door.

Who could it be on a Friday?

He headed to the door only to discover…a delivery service?

"Sign here?"

He nodded as he took the box in his hands, bringing it

into the house. A quick slip of his knife and he opened it to discover a card and a bag, marked with the C's Place logo.

Lifting the bag out first, he saw…a challah?

Then he pulled out the card. There had to be some explanation.

Dear Abe,

I really appreciate the ice cream, and I'm not going to do this every time you send me a package, although you have to admit that this is a pretty obvious response gift.

But I am not responding to your gift with this; this is a thank you. I saw you in the auditorium and I appreciated your support more than words could say. She didn't bring her raisin challahs to the class, but I figured you'd appreciate this one.

Batya

Of all the explanations he could have expected for a challah showing up at his door, this was the very last one. Yet the way it made him feel was second to none.

At some point he'd have to bite the bullet and talk about the graduation party with her, but for the moment, he was enjoying the bridge that food was building between them.

Chapter Ten

ONCE AGAIN, THE weekend had passed, and it was Wednesday. And at 5:45, she'd finished her matzah ball soup and felt ready to start the class. But she wasn't terrified. Maybe it was because she'd spent time with her aunt and had coffee with Claire and hadn't spent the weekend focusing on the class. Who knew?

What she did know was that Jacob and Anna were supposed to arrive at 6:05, and the second she saw her watch turn over, she heard footsteps and looked up to see her friends had arrived on time.

"We brought you tea," Anna said with a smile, handing over the cup. "You didn't get a chance to drink the last one so we stopped at the Caf and Nosh and brought you more."

"Oh, you guys," she said as she put the cup on the lectern and reached out for a hug.

"We figured you could use some extra, more tangible support."

"Thank you," she said, slightly overcome by the gesture. "This is…"

"Friends, family," Jacob said as Anna nodded. "This is

what we do."

But of course, that was when Abe walked into the room, taking a pause in his step, smiling in her direction. She smiled back at him before he headed up the steps to his seat.

"What," Anna said with a grin, "is that?"

"Nice?"

"Nice?" Anna asked as she met Jacob's eyes. He squeezed her hand, let it go and saluted before he headed up the stairs. "Now, you should probably tell me about this *nice*, but like not now because we have class."

And for some reason, the good feeling Batya'd had before the class started didn't wane or dissipate. It continued and strengthened.

She could do this.

And definitely not spill that mint tea all over herself.

ONCE AGAIN, ABE came into the auditorium to discover that Batya was chatting with some vaguely familiar people at the front. Once again, he didn't want to interrupt, but all the same he smiled at her, making sure she saw him before he headed up to his usual seat.

As he settled in, pulling out his notes and notebook, he heard: "Oooh. Great. Someone sitting here?"

Abe turned to find…Jacob?

Was that his name?

"No," he said, "help yourself."

"Good," the other man said in a way that made it obvious he'd expected to be welcomed.

"Knock yourself out," Abe said with a smile. Though curiosity started to seep in after he'd thought about it. What would a Hollowville friend of Batya's want with him?

"I don't need it for very long," the man continued as he settled into the seat, "because I'm going to be display assistant number one tonight, but the lecturer needed to chat with the organizer, which is what finds me here. With you." He paused. "Abe?"

And just like that, Abe instantly felt better about not remembering the other man's name. "That's me," he said. "Abe Newman."

"Jacob," the other man said. Smooth. Not the scary shark he'd met back on the day of Batya's audition. This was someone else. "Nice to meet you again."

Abe took the hand the other man offered.

"How was the dry cleaning bill?" Jacob asked.

Ahhh. So this was a follow up conversation from the night of the audition. Fair enough. "She balked."

He raised an eyebrow. "And you?"

Abe didn't want to go into details, but there was enough he could say that he was okay with. "I suggested something else, and she accepted."

Jacob nodded, and Abe remembered that, right now, the other man was here as a friend of Batya's. "Good. Very good."

And in the silence, Abe wasn't quite sure what to say.

"I'm impressed, actually."

Abe raised an eyebrow. "Why?"

"Why am I impressed, or why am I interested?"

Was this an interrogation? Evaluation? It was time to find out. "Either," he said. "Both."

"Batya's Anna's friend," Jacob replied, beginning with what he clearly felt was the most salient point. "You vex her. She doesn't vex."

Again. Made sense. If he'd known Batya separately from her time in Rivertown, he'd probably see a different Batya, the same way the people who knew him when he was in Binghamton for college, or Boston for grad school knew a different Abe.

"And, I figure there are things you need to fix."

From calming and chatting to…advice? "I'm not following."

"Tony told me he saw you, which was good. But also, and here's the important part, you didn't give up when she didn't agree to the dry cleaning."

So this was both an interrogation and an evaluation. "Okay?"

"That, and that moment where she was completely and utterly calm despite the very obvious panic attack Tony told me about the week before, means there's something deeper going on between you than just dry cleaning bills."

Still didn't make sense. This was a labyrinth, where each turn sent him more off balance than the last. Not the chaos kind of confusion he usually dealt with from Artur; at least that was familiar. This was someone trying to tie together a whole bunch of unrelated events because he was looking out for Batya, trying to make a friend, or thought that Batya had feelings for him and so Jacob was judging him.

No.

Couldn't go down that route.

Who did that though? An *analyst*, that's who. But it was still confusing.

"Hold that thought. I'm being signaled." Jacob reached into his pocket. "Text me," he said as he passed over a thick business card, which Abe took. "We'll talk more. Plan to talk about"—the other man gestured—"things."

Abe wasn't sure how to respond, so he simply said thank you as Batya walked up to the front of the room.

"Okay, everybody," Batya began, much more confident than she'd been the week before. "Welcome to tonight's lecture. Just to remind everybody, we are live. The lecture will also be available after tonight, on the fry-off website, foodworld.com, and for tonight's lecture only, mmjh.org. Which brings us to tonight's lecturer."

Abe settled back into his chair. This, he decided, was going to be good.

"Anna Cohen is a curator for special projects based out of the Manhattan Museum of Jewish History. Her focus is on Eastern European Jewish history and the history of Jewish social justice movements in the United States. She has also worked a bit with the history of German Jewry in the United States. She's here to talk about the mythology associated with kosher food, and Jewish-American food in general. Let's welcome Anna."

And just as he'd predicted, Jacob stood, heading to the aisle, carrying a large box, which the other man displayed to the room as if he were an assistant on a game show. Of course, Abe couldn't miss the indulgent expression on Anna's face. And Batya's slight headshake.

"So who here has heard the myth that Jewish-American food, especially Ashkenazi food, is bland, boring, and inedible? Raise a hand please."

How many times had he heard that this week? This year? He raised his hand.

"Okay," the lecturer continued. "Who has ever used wasabi on their sushi?"

He wasn't sure where she was headed, but he raised his hand anyway.

"Good. Here's the tie you're looking for: who in this audience has a jar of pastel-colored horseradish in their fridge? Pink, purple—any color. Come on. We know it. It's the first thing most of us from Ashkenazi households look for in fridges."

That's when Abe got it.

Chrain.

Chrain was horseradish dyed in beet juice. He put it on

gefilte fish and on so many other things.

He raised his hand along with everybody else.

The lecturer smiled and stood, flipping over the white-board to reveal a detailed outline. "All of you get the idea. We do spice our food. We do make it flavorful. But food *spice* is different for us. Necessitated by the fact that food preparation is, and has always been, different for us. And this is what we're going to talk about. My assistant"—she waved her hand at Jacob, who bowed—"and I are going to dispel the myths, clarify the truth, and remind you that Jewish food, no matter where it comes from, has a strong tradition of both comforting and feeding an oppressed people."

And as Abe started to take notes, he couldn't help but watch Batya. The change between last week and this one was remarkable. She spoke without having to force herself to, she was able to sit and relax, dropping her shoulders. She was even taking *notes* instead of focusing on how she'd end the lecture. It was simply impressive.

Her hands were still shaking, and she was taking long sips from that huge plastic cup during the moments where she wasn't speaking, but she seemed to have found her way. He could see her name in lights, if a show she found fasci-nated her as much as this one. He knew she could do it.

But could he? Could he figure out the latke recipes, and pull together a plan for what he wanted? Could he manage to talk to her about graduation?

All he did know is that he'd decided what ice cream Batya was going to get next, and that maybe, when he got around to it, he'd call Jacob.

ON THURSDAY MORNING, Batya was doing a deep dive of her notes for the blog when the doorbell rang. Once again, it was the ice cream shop.

"Delivery from Rivertown Ice."

Batya smiled. "Ahhh, yes. Thank you."

She took the box into the house once again, cut it open with a pair of scissors, and removed the cooling packs.

Once again, she shoved her childlike impulse to dive right into the ice cream to the side. Adults read cards first, and she was starting to anticipate the card as much as the ice cream.

Dear Batya,

Salt is an important part of Jewish cuisine, for sure, from the beginning where you use it to kosher meat and as a spice—placed in soups and other things.

But we also sweeten life; we make sweet kugel and sweet gefilte fish.

In other words, we make sweet the bitter and make bitter the sweet.

Enjoy this ice cream that does a great job of tying these two things together.

Abe

Salted caramel. Two for two.

Did she have to send him something too?

Had to? Wanted to?

Both.

⫸⚹⫷

FRIDAY MORNING CAME, and once again Abe was prepping for his barbecue. Chicken too, because Claire hadn't stopped pestering him. Two different sauces, two different rubs, which meant he had to start early.

The doorbell rang.

Once again, it was one of the package services.

This box was smaller.

As he opened it, he saw a thick vacuum bag containing kosher salt. The label was from a spice company he'd been dying to try but hadn't managed yet. And then he opened the card.

Dear Abe,

I told you I wasn't going to send you response gifts every single time, but apparently this time I also can't help myself. This company is fantastic, and I'd gotten an email from them about one of the projects they're working on with the Mitzvah Alliance and Katie Feldman's Helping Hands charity; I couldn't help but support it and them.

You're just the beneficiary of my choices. Bask in

that, Abe, just like you let me bask in your smile during class. Enjoy.

Batya

He found himself smiling, and realized how lucky he was.

Food was fixing what an ill-advised drunken moment had torn asunder.

All he had to do was actually make amends before things, and cookies, crumbled before his eyes.

Chapter Eleven

SATURDAY WAS GOING well. The sides were on the stove, and the meats were almost ready; both the beef and the freshly added chicken were almost at their peak cooking times.

Artur had been telling him a story about his parents, and their thwarted ambition to go to one of the research bases on Antarctica, which sent them to Australia instead.

"They're really enjoying this year of voyages thing."

Artur smiled. "Making up for what they didn't do during their youth and then when I was a kid."

"I really admire them, you know. Seeing the world, loving every second of it."

Artur raised an eyebrow. "Your father is also doing this, so I'm not sure why my parents' journey without a plan fascinates you more than your father's never-ending cruise."

Abe laughed. "Context. Dad's not gotten off the ship once."

"You're serious?"

Abe nodded. "Yeah. He's in these great places and all he's doing is staring at the daily towel animal. Don't get it either."

"Speaking of things I don't get," Artur said as he pulled out a fork. "Did you call him?"

Abe did not have any idea why he'd made the mistake of telling Artur about the business card burning a hole in his wallet. But he had, probably in a moment of searching for connection. And he figured Artur would be able to give him advice, or at least sympathize.

He also expected the ribbing about it.

He did not expect his friend to take up nagging like the neighborhood nudnik he sometimes was.

The answer, of course, was the same as it had been. "No."

Artur shook his head. "I don't understand you. You're being a coward."

Maybe Artur was right. Maybe he was being a coward. But the problem was easily explained. "I don't know what he's after and he's just intimidating."

"Intimidating? You still talk to me," Artur pointed out as he continued to stir the mashed potatoes. "And you know you find me—"

"Infuriating, not intimidating."

"Same difference. Just a bit more annoyance than awe tied to the emotions. You should try thinking of me as intimidating. See how that feels."

That made Abe laugh. "No," he said once he'd stopped laughing. "You're not intimidating. Not at all."

"Which," Artur continued as he took a long drink of his soda, "is the point. We've known each other since I was a snot-nosed fifth grader. Still the same attitude, but a bunch less awe because, again, snot-nosed, Coke bottle glasses, and an accent big enough to ride. You've seen me at my worst, so you're not in awe of me."

Abe shook his head. "I also know better than to be in awe of you. It'll make that ego of yours worse than it usually is."

"I," Artur replied, "have no ego. But that guy? The one you don't want to call, with the card way too many people in the city, if not the world, would love to have? I'm sure someone's seen him with snot running down his nose, hm?"

Which made Abe feel a little better. Not better enough to call the guy, but better about thinking about it. "I guess…"

Artur shook his head. "You mean I'm right. But what I also am is hungry. We've been cooking all afternoon, and you haven't fed me any of this amazing hickory-smoked gorgeousness."

So, per usual, Abe rolled his eyes and prepared to take the meat out of the smoker. "And I thought you came here for the fellowship."

"No. I came for the food," Artur replied, laughing. And then he paused, gave him a look that meant business. "Just promise me you'll make that call before someone else tells you, 'kay?"

"Who says I told anybody else?" he told his friend. "But yes. I promise to think about it. And to feed you."

Artur nodded, and that made him feel better. For now.

BATYA HAD RELAXED a bit before the class where she'd spent the weekend reconnecting with friends and family, as opposed to staying inside and in her head. Which made sense, of course. More time outside doing things meant less time analyzing things that had already happened.

All of that reminded her how much she'd enjoyed having coffee with Claire the weekend before. So she called and asked her friend if she wanted to get together.

"Of course I do," Claire said when presented with the question. "I am always up for it."

Two coffees from the Bean Barn later, they were sitting back at the kitchen table. "So how are you doing? I love the website, by the way."

"Thanks. It's been nice but also somewhat strange, you know?"

"So many memories around this table," Claire said, nodding. Claire had transferred to public school when Batya had, and Batya was there when Claire had broken up with her first girlfriend.

"But," Claire continued, "it's great to be back here. I missed you."

"Missed you too. So, aside from the restaurant disaster, what's been going on here in RT?"

Claire grinned. This was going to be interesting.

"Are you getting barbecue this weekend?" she asked. "Have you tried it?"

"I haven't tried it," Batya admitted. "But I'm starting to think I should at least see what the fuss is about."

"Well, you are in luck." Claire beamed. Whether her friend was oblivious or not in the mood to poke between Batya's words, Batya wasn't sure. Either way, she'd gotten a reprieve from her usually inquisitive friend.

"Oh really," Batya found herself saying. "Any particular reason?"

"Yeah. I got some for this week," Claire continued. "Figured I had to especially because he's finally making chicken."

Batya laughed. "Yeah. You absolutely had to. What did he do? Email you and tell you?"

"Pretty much." Claire shook her head. "Anyway, I got way too much. So you're going to share with me. Dinner either here or at my place?"

Was her luck changing?

She'd started to think it was necessary to try Abe's barbecue, and now it was about to drop in her lap, courtesy of one very good friend. "That sounds perfect."

"Good. I have to tell you, I was getting nervous that I'd have to have leftovers for a month."

"That's a problem?" Batya asked.

Claire shook her head. "No. Not really. Just…you'll see."

Unfortunately, life was never that easy because there she was, a few hours later, sitting in Claire's car as her friend tried to find a spot in front of Abe's house.

"You're going to love it. I promise you," Claire said.

"Promises, promises." Batya sat back against the front passenger seat, trying not to stare inside Abe's house. She knew she'd love his cooking; he was too focused on food and flavor to make her think otherwise. But she was still walking a dangerous line. The last thing she wanted was to encourage emotions that were still fascinated by him.

But she asked anyway. "So, what's his deal?"

"What do you mean?"

"I mean, why is he here? Why is he back living—?"

"In his childhood house, like some other people are?"

She snorted. "Looow blow, MacLeish. So what's the deal? Why?"

Claire shrugged. "His father finally retired. Abe moved back and took over the house…two years ago? Now his dad's on the trip around the world he'd always wanted to take and sends Abe pictures."

"That's nice," Batya said. "I can't even make something weird about that because I'm house-sitting for snowbirds."

Claire laughed. "I can only guess how weird it is for you. If you stay, you'll have to get a place."

If she stayed, she'd have to get herself a place.

That was a thought.

Not living with Tante Shelly in Hollowville or borrowing Anna's old apartment in Brooklyn or…

"I didn't ask you to solve the world's problems," Claire said. "I only mentioned a place to live."

Settling down. Somewhere.

"I'll figure it out," she said. "Anyway, how does this work?"

"Roll down the window," Claire replied, accepting the change of subject way too easily. "You're about to find out."

She rolled the window down and turned to see…

"Abe."

"In the flesh, with your order, Claire."

"Ooooh," her friend replied, her eyes dancing, visions of barbecue chicken dancing in her eyes. "Excellent. Send me the invoice, and I'll—"

Abe shook his head. "This one," he said turning to meet Batya's eyes, "is on the house."

Batya wanted to nip that in the bud immediately. She didn't want him to give her free food because she'd decided to order. "Not on my account, please."

"This is my treat," he insisted, and she recognized that voice. That *I'm going to be stubborn for the rest of my life because I've decided* voice.

What would that voice sound like…?

"Batya."

His voice broke into her ridiculously dumb daydreams. "Right. Sorry." She tried not to react when her hand brushed his as she took the bag from his grasp.

Tried not to look up at him and see his nonreaction when their hands brushed.

And tried to remember that she did *not* want to get herself entangled with him again, or get her hopes up about him again.

"Thanks," she said.

"No problem."

And then Claire rolled up the window, gave Abe a quick wave goodbye as Batya tried not to watch him standing on the lawn, watching them drive away.

Dammit.

ABE SPENT SATURDAY night and most of Sunday wondering what Batya had thought of his barbecue. He tried to forget the way his hand burned when he gave her the bag.

The last thing he wanted was to instigate any romantic or other sort of drama with Batya. Nope.

No matter how he felt.

He couldn't call her, email her, or ask her directly in any way. He didn't want to put pressure on her. Or anybody who'd observed her reactions to his food.

Which meant he wasn't going to call Claire and give her the third degree. Nope.

Nor was he going to call any of the other members of the

group to find out if they'd heard about Saturday night's barbecue experience.

Mostly because the last thing he wanted to do was find out she hated it. If nothing else, he didn't want to see the reactions from the rest of the quiz bowl team. It would be a disaster.

Instead, on Monday, he forced himself to turn back to the numbers that he was working on. There were bits of taxes he had to finish and send to his boss, as well as the basic progress report about what was happening with the fry-off.

Finally, the last set of numbers were done, and he attached the spreadsheet to the document before hitting send on the email.

Now what?

He'd made lunch, eaten it, pondered what he was doing later and the experimentation he had to do with his spice rub.

Which meant everything was done with the exception of finally using the card in his pocket.

Jacob Horowitz-Margareten.

The man had searched for answers and something else last Wednesday night. Maybe he could do the same. Could he find out what Batya had been like in Hollowville? Maybe she'd let it slip what she thought of his barbecue?

Maybe the guy was looking for a friend. He could do with a friend. Especially a friend Artur had said would be a good idea to contact. Artur was many things, but he was very, very good at judging people, whether it was because of his job or whether it was because of who he was in general.

He pulled out the card, brushed his finger against the heavy cardstock.

A 516 area code on the phone, Long Island.

The guy said to text. Okay.

He blew out a breath.

To: 516-555-2222
From: 914-555-2351

Hi. It's Abe Newman. Sorry it took so long to text. Looking forward to chatting further.

He sent the text, put his phone down, and checked his email. And of course, a bunch of new emails meant more to take care of. But just as he sat down, he heard the phone buzzing against the table.

From: 516-555-2222
To: 914-555-2351

Good to hear from you, Abe. Sending you three times I can talk; let me know which one works for you. Looking forward to it!!!
Jacob

Abe had never seen so many exclamation points in a text before in his life, but he went with it and picked a time. Judging by the card, and a few other things, this guy was operating at a different level than most of the people he met, even some he worked with. Though how different, and whether it was a good different or a bad different, remained to be seen.

From: 516-555-2222
To: 914-555-2351

Sounds good. Send me the name of a restaurant by you, and we'll have lunch. I'll be on my way to Hollowville from the Island anyway, so I can stop by.
Looking forward to it.

Jacob

Which meant he'd be having lunch at Leo's with this guy.

One thing he could say was that the late lunch was going to be interesting, no matter what he or Jacob were going to be fishing for.

Chapter Twelve

ON WEDNESDAY, BATYA headed to class and found herself in a situation she did not expect. She'd had plans with Chana to talk before class, and then ended up going with Chana into the auditorium, only to find Linda—George Gold's assistant—sitting by herself, on the opposite side of the auditorium from where Abe usually sat. Unlike her, Linda was comfortable, dark hair atop her head in a perfect chignon.

If Batya had managed to calm down with the help of a conversation with Chana and her sweet tea, that went out the window the second she saw Linda.

Her hands were shaking, and making it through the first part of the class where she introduced Chana was almost impossible. Thankfully, she was reading from notes she'd memorized.

She somehow managed to put up a finger and exited the room, leaving the lecture in Chana's hands.

Even as the sweat started to pour down the back of her neck.

She couldn't breathe.

She headed through the corridor, past the auditorium, to the open quadrangle area. It had been covered over, but it was still the school's link to the outside, the separation between the back end of the gym and auditorium and the rest of the space.

She slipped through the old door and entered into this small patch of the outside, trying desperately to calm down.

ABE HAD INTENDED to learn about the world of dairy from Chana when he arrived at the high school that day.

Chana had owned a restaurant in Hollowville for years, and he wondered how she did it, how a dairy restaurant survived in the next town over but the deli didn't survive in Rivertown.

Things to ask about.

He was also wondering how Batya liked the food he'd made. Even was prepared to joke about it when he came in. Tried three different variations of a joke. But as he walked into the room, he could tell something was amiss, and any joke he had prepared went out the window.

Batya was sitting on the desk, and the woman who had to be Chana paced in front of the whiteboard. Unlike the almost vivacious host she'd been the week before, Batya was as pale as chalk.

He stopped to wave at her, then realized she wasn't focusing on anything, just staring out at the upper tier of seats.

Knowing that it mattered, knowing that she mattered, he waved at her anyway before heading upstairs to his seat.

What the heck had happened to make her so nervous?

He settled into his seat, and then he noticed the woman who sat in the very back row. By herself, in the chignon. Nobody else in that room was sitting anywhere near her, and this wasn't a situation where a VIP from Hollowville was sitting there.

And if this woman's presence was enough to send Batya into a tailspin, he needed to be on guard. Glad that he was sitting on the same level with one of the auditorium's many exits, and even better that it was literally steps away from where he sat.

When Batya left the room, he waited a few seconds to disguise his intentions as best he could, and then he left too. As he slipped into the hallway, he realized that there was only one place she could go. He hoped that she'd be okay when he found her.

THE SWEAT WAS rolling down Batya's neck as she sat down on the old bench. The plants had all died; they were rotted and the planters rusted, but the space was still there. Just like it had been all those years ago when she attended Rivertown High School.

Thank God they hadn't locked the door.

At least that was going her way. She tried to focus on something and failed.

All she knew was the never-ending circle of panic.

"You okay?"

Batya looked up, trying desperately to focus on something beyond the sound of his voice.

And yet it didn't matter. She knew it was Abe. He'd seen her at her best; he'd even given her a massage at the audition. He deserved the truth. "No," she said.

"May I?"

Batya understood immediately what Abe was asking her. She'd asked him to give her a massage at the audition, both before she went on stage and after. But she was so chilled, so scared now, that she was barely capable of nodding. Even as his hands settled on her shoulders, she felt the pressure, but couldn't lean in to the heat of his touch.

"What's going to happen," he said, his voice wrapping around her like a fuzzy blanket, as she felt his fingers start to work her muscles, "is that we're going to sit here for a little. However long you need."

"I can't," she managed, pulling words out from her lips when she could barely focus. Not just because his hands were making their way around her, making her shoulder muscles feel like liquid. But because she'd lost so much by leaving. She could lose the show, lose the chance to host…

"So, we'll sit here till you can," he said.

His voice was something she could focus on. His voice and the easy rhythm of his fingertips.

"Keep talking," she managed. "Please."

"You're just benefitting from my good choices," he said in a way that indicated she was supposed to laugh or even remember why what he'd said was funny. Wait...

Was it from the note she'd sent him with the salt?

Yes. That's what it was.

"And my need to stretch," he continued, not pausing for a second, to her endless relief. "When you're feeling better, you'll head back, to the backstage. Come in and through the stairs, you know?"

She did. He was telling her to enter the lecture hall the way she came in to her audition. "And you?"

"I'll go up through the back and come in near my seat."

At least one of them was thinking, at least one of them had a clear picture of life in his mind.

She smiled back at him, able to match the speed of her breath to his, in the way they always suggested on one of those meditation tapes. It was one of the most amazing, most thrilling moments she'd ever had.

"Thank you," she said, taking his hand for a very brief second before leaving the room and running off to the auditorium.

"You're welcome."

ONCE HE GOT back to the room, Abe could tell that Batya was doing a little better. Albeit shakily as she held on to the podium tight enough that her knuckles were white.

But unfortunately, the woman with the chignon was sitting with her arms folded, clearly angry.

He couldn't do anything about it. He wished he could fix it, wished that someone could make this woman, whoever she was, see how brilliant Batya had always been. And how much people were pulling for her. That one moment where Batya had needed to leave the room to get herself under control wasn't the only moment that mattered when it came to her ability to host a television show. Or the fry-off.

"Next week," Batya managed, "will be the meat portion, where a titan of the kosher meat restaurant industry will be in to talk about cooking kosher meat, and what makes meat kosher."

For whatever reason, that was when the entire room, except the woman with the chignon, got up and applauded.

And with this woman's eyes on him, he was very happy to stand up and join them.

WHEN THE CLASS was over, Batya sent Abe a brief text telling him she'd call him later. The very last thing she needed was anybody there to watch her break down in front of Linda.

"All I'm going to say," Linda said as she came down the stairs, "is that you absolutely need to hold this together. One more incident like this, and I will have no choice but to find another host. I know you have stage fright, but there are tons of other people available who can put this show on flawlessly. George might love your blog, and he might appreciate your concept, but this is his name you're riding on. You can't go up there and lose control of a lecture and yourself. If you do this in front of him, you're going to ruin his name."

Batya nodded. This was less than she expected, much more than she deserved. "I…"

"The only reason you're still here," Linda said, "is that you nailed the second episode. Nailed it. Completely. This is unacceptable. One more screw-up, and you're done."

Once again, not able to find any other reaction, Batya nodded. "Right."

She *absolutely* understood.

Her life was on the verge of collapse and she had to hold herself together.

Only when she got home did she start to cry. Because if she'd sobbed in front of anybody else, she would not have been able to stop.

The next morning, she pulled herself together. There were more classes to prepare for, friends she couldn't let down.

Goals she couldn't lose sight of.

And a whole bunch of things she had to deal with

around the house for her snowbird parents.

Coffee didn't solve everything, but it was warm, soothing and inviting, the place where she started her day. About halfway through her first cup, just as she had pulled out her notebook and a pen to make her to-do list, there was a knock at the door. She wondered what Abe had sent her this time.

Because of course, the delivery person wore the Rivertown Ice garb, the cooler he carried bright blue, and full of reasons to smile.

Once again she brought in the box, placing it on the table.

This time, what she needed most was to see the letter.

Batya,

My first thought was that the tea you were drinking yesterday was mint, and so I was going to send you mint chocolate chip. Except if I'm not mistaken, that was the stuff I spilled on you back at the beginning of this whole adventure of ours.

So I'm not going to send you something so poignant. Instead, I'm going to send you something funny, so that you can be the beneficiary of my good decisions. (And yes. Good decisions. I was surprised at how good this stuff tasted when I tried it.)

If you'd like to be the beneficiary of more of my good decisions, and want to learn more about my homemade barbecue sauce, as well as see how I use it, consider this your invitation to visit me on Saturday. Come at 1:00, have lunch with me, and I'll tell you the story of my barbecue.

Abe

As she sat back against her poor kitchen chair, holding a container of "everything bagel swirl" ice cream she smiled.

She could do this. She'd be ready.

ON THURSDAY AFTERNOON, Abe pulled into the parking lot of Fratelli's about ten minutes before he was supposed to meet Jacob. There were a few spaces in the lot, and he opted for one toward the back, farthest away from the entrance and people who had no idea how to park. He stretched, got out of the car.

But the question remained as to what exactly was happening here.

For himself, Abe was prepared for anything; but when it came down to it, he wanted to ask Jacob what he knew about Batya.

But what did Jacob want?

Was this a conversation about business? A cursory internet search showed Jacob Horowitz-Margareten ran multiple funds that focused on charitable and zero-interest grants, had more business interests than most people had credit cards, and a portfolio focusing on startups meant to serve underserved communities, among other things. The width and breadth of the man's holdings would scare most investment advisors he knew. On top of all of that, he had ties to two major charitable organizations the rumor mill said he actually ran.

All of which? Honestly? Looked oddly familiar to his tax accountant's eyes.

But he was also a friend by proxy of Batya's, so was this going to be a conversation where he warned him away from Batya, friend's fiancé to friend?

Was this an opening salvo in a friendship?

Would it be all of these or none of them?

Would Jacob even show up?

If worst came to worst, he'd bother Leo for a late lunch. Friendship had its privileges.

But, of course, he looked up to see a black sedan pull into the lot. It was sleek and desperately trying not to look as flashy or as expensive as it probably was, not like his own random "oh crap, I need a car" purchase of two years before.

The car pulled into the space next to his, easily, as if the driver actually knew how to drive. Which was a random thing to think about, but how many of these cars were driven by people who weren't their owners?

"You can't grow up on Long Island and not know how to drive," came the voice as the driver's side door opened. "Good to see you."

"Good to be seen," he replied, smiling. "Shall we?"

Jacob smiled back as he hit the lock button. "We shall."

"Place is quiet now," Abe said as they headed toward the restaurant. "The owner's setting up for dinner, but because I've known him forever, he's letting us have a late lunch. And again, old friend, so I've been eating his food since before he could cook."

"Iron stomach or…?"

Abe shook his head. The last impression he wanted to give was that Leo wasn't a good cook. "Best critic," he finally said as they walked into the restaurant, "is someone who knows you well enough to tell you what you need to hear, not what you want to. I figure someone who's known me since kindergarten isn't going to be annoyed if I tell him he didn't put enough pepper in his soup."

Jacob laughed. "True."

"Stop with the pepper," Leo yelled as he emerged from the kitchen. "It was one soup, and I was ten."

"Leo," he said, "this is Jacob, a friend of Batya's. Jacob, this is Leo, who's taken over this restaurant and who I have known since both of us could barely read."

Leo nodded. "It's true. My wife is working at her family's place at the moment. *She* thinks I should use more pepper."

"A smidge of horseradish would make everything better," Abe quipped, their traditional routine never taking the day off.

"And all of your whining about how different cuisines require different spices goes out the window just because you want to torture me," Leo said. "Just in case you thought I wasn't listening."

"He really doesn't listen," Abe said, shaking his head. "He just puts it on for show."

And of all the things he expected from Jacob, the laugh, as if he'd been hanging around them for all of his life, was not it. "Oh," Jacob said, "this is going to be amazing."

And it was. Homemade pasta, lasagna, and the good stuff Leo didn't put on the menu but indulged his friends in every once in a while.

"This is fantastic," Jacob said, taking a long swig from his glass of water. "I am impressed."

"He's showing off," Abe replied. "But seriously. This is comfort food at its best."

Jacob nodded, and Abe wasn't sure what the expression was. "I like. Thanks. You're probably wondering why I wanted to meet you here."

"Partially."

He nodded. "You work at Waxman?"

"I'm on leave from Waxman. Mr. Lieb is sponsoring my adventures in latke fry-offs. Except for one project he's got me on."

"I'm guessing that the project he's got you on is mine."

Abe shrugged. "Maybe? I don't know."

"I talked to Lieb," he replied. "So *I* do. You're taking care of the complex mess that is my taxes, and for that I'm grateful."

This was the independent republic? No wonder the portfolio he saw when he searched looked familiar.

No wonder Batya was snorting when he was joking about his client at dinner the first night she'd been back in town.

He was glad he didn't have anything in his mouth. Just the same, it was difficult to pull himself together and make sure he hadn't dropped his jaw on the table.

"Okay."

"But that's not why I'm here."

So why? What was this?

"First," Jacob said, "you seem like a nice guy who's in a bit of a weird spot."

Abe shrugged. "Sure. I guess."

"Freaking someone out enough by just breathing that they covered themselves in tea is something I've had experience in, though in my case it was flour and sugar."

Ahhh. That weird spot. Relationships. Batya.

But Abe sure as hell couldn't hide the disbelief, so he'd go with it. And, as Artur said, everybody was a snot-nosed kid once.

And somehow part of that disbelief dissipated enough to be able to joke about it. "You're kidding?"

Jacob laughed. "'Fraid not. I was dealing with stress by folding bourekas in the prep room at my friend's bakery, and when I went to announce that I'd finished, there, in front of the counter, was someone I hadn't seen in five months, someone I desperately missed."

"What happened?"

"Gets worse, of course."

Abe shook his head. "How is that possible?"

"Because of boundaries I'd set with this person," Jacob answered, "I left my friend's bakery covered in flour and sugar, possibly butter."

"Holy crap." Abe paused, realizing how judgmental his reaction might have been. "I mean," he managed. "How did you resolve that?"

The smile on Jacob's face was brighter than anything he'd ever seen. It wasn't smug. It was happy. "She and I are getting married in less than six months."

"You're kidding."

Jacob shook his head. "No, definitely not. This isn't something I joke about."

There was a steel in Jacob's eyes. The one Abe had seen before, at the audition. "So you're here to help with romantic advice?"

"Partially." Jacob shrugged. "Romantic advice, business advice."

"Why business advice?"

"Because anybody who enters a latke fry-off, makes really good barbecue on the weekends, and gets offered a sponsorship from the tax firm they're working at for said fry-off clearly needs advice."

Despite the fact that it raised so many questions, like

how Jacob had tasted his barbecue, Abe had to admit the other man's assessment was dead on. Abe needed to get a handle on the situation before he said something embarrassing. "What advice do you think I need?"

"How conflicted are you?"

"Excuse me?"

"Let me step back a second," Jacob said after pausing to drink some more of his water. "Do you know what you want?"

"I know what I'd like," Abe replied after thinking for a second. The navigation path of the conversation was so very beyond him. "I just don't know if it's possible."

"Which means you're not conflicted, just stuck."

"Stuck?"

Jacob nodded. "Something's holding you back. What is it?"

Abe sat back against his seat, taking a breadstick in the process. "I hate to break it to you, but doing a specifically Jewish restaurant, a deli, is expensive, and the industry…"

"Yes," Jacob interrupted, an expression of what looked like boredom framing his face. "This particular segment of the industry is seen by many as a risk at best, a really awful decision at worst, fueled by both gentilification—a term my ancestors would be less than proud to hear coming from my mouth—and homogenization of the industry as well as rising rent and you name it. Yes. I know."

Once again, the boundaries of the conversation had

shifted. And he felt like he was at some weird crossroad. "Yeah. Didn't mean it like that."

Jacob shook his head. "It's fine. I'm an analyst by trade, so I always come prepared to talk business, even though I don't usually end up spouting off whatever statistics I've found."

"Practical accountant," Abe replied, gesturing at himself with the half-eaten breadstick. "You ask about my dreams, and the problem is, I can't see past the numbers—not that I don't think you don't know them."

"So then let's force ourselves past the numbers, or at least talk about the heart of the issue."

Abe nodded. "I like that." He put the breadstick down and reached to clink Jacob's water glass.

"Excellent," Jacob said. "Here's the thing. People are starting to rediscover a need for a truly Jewish-American cuisine. To find our roots in food in ways that we can't, or frankly don't want, to spend the time preparing ourselves. Not elevated—dear God, if I had a penny for everybody who said they were elevating Ashkenazi cuisine. My fiancée does the research; I get fascinated by anything she researches, always have. And the problem with anybody trying to open something these days is that they don't know the history. You do."

Abe raised an eyebrow. "What are you telling me?"

Jacob smiled. "I don't invest in friends, because things get awkward way too quickly. Especially when they're newer friends. Less water under the bridge, fewer incidents where we've both seen each other in compromising situations."

Apparently this was Jacob's equivalent of Artur's snot-nosed kids standard. "Which makes sense," Abe replied because it needed to be said. "But I wasn't asking that. I'm trying to figure what kind of advice you're giving me, because I don't mix friendship with business either."

"Another reason why I like you." A smile, a bit more relaxed, as if Jacob had judged him and found him worthy. "But what I can, and will, do for a friend is get you talking to people who might teach you things. So you can make informed decisions no matter what happens at that competition."

"What do you mean, informed decisions?"

"You know the numbers, the end result. What I suspect you don't know are the specifics behind the scenes, the nitty-gritty nature of the kosher/Jewish deli business. It's hard work. Really hard work. *That*, I can get you insight into."

"I appreciate it." Abe found himself smiling. "I very much appreciate it." He paused. "And I'm looking forward to hanging out more."

"Hopefully, you're a hockey fan. And if not, especially if you play your cards right with Batya, we'll be spending a lot of time together."

Hockey, huh. This was a salvo he was ready for. "I am so excited to watch Ben Klein score another fifty goals."

"And you are very lucky I'm an Empires fan. Do you

think Carly Emerson makes the jump this year?"

Abe relaxed and had started to explain the reasons why he thought the Empires were going to end up as the first MHL team with a female goaltender when there was a loud buzzing sound.

Jacob shook his head, grabbed his phone. And swore. "I have to take this," he said, leaving the table. And leaving his jacket behind.

As Abe had no idea what was happening, he turned his brain toward what he could control, the things he had to take care of before the weekend's barbecue, if Batya was going to take him up on his offer...

"She's about to lose the class." Jacob's voice was clear as he walked back into the room, as if he were speaking about something that was a foregone conclusion. "I'm going to have to go and make a few phone calls. Do you have any ideas?"

Abe blinked. "What? Excuse me?"

Jacob nodded, sat back down. "Right. Let me get you up to speed. Anna called me, which is why I answered, expecting an emergency. Anyway." He took a long drink from his glass of water. "To make a long story short, Batya was threatened with losing the class."

"Yeah. Last night."

"This morning, her main lecturer for next week canceled."

"Dammit."

"Dammit is right," Jacob said with a shake of his head. "So Batya wants to take me up on an offer I made her for a potential replacement lecture when she was organizing the class, which means I now have to track someone down. I may have to go grab Anna and then drive back to the Island, so I need to head out." He paused. "And even though I don't like to have to say this, I may not manage to convince this guy. Which means I need backup."

Backup?

"You want me to come with you?"

Jacob shook his head. "This is something I have to take care of on my own, though I do appreciate the offer."

"Not a problem. But what did you mean, exactly?"

"If I don't manage this," Jacob replied, "and even if I do, you're a barbecue guy. You must know someone who isn't you who knows a thing or two about kosher meat."

"She's not going to call me," he said. "She's really not going to call me."

Jacob looked at him. "She might surprise you. Reach out if she doesn't."

And just as he was about to tell Jacob, for the third time, that there was no way Batya would ask him for help, his phone buzzed against the table.

A text.

He looked at the message. It was from Batya, of course, asking him to call her when he could. "I guess I have to make a call."

Jacob smiled. "I guess you do."

"This is on me," Abe said as he swiped the paper printout off the plastic holder as if to end the conversation. "Next time I might let you pay, but we're not setting a tone for this friendship by having you pay the first time."

"Fair enough."

After they finished the business of paying, Abe walked Jacob to the parking lot. "Good luck," he said.

"Thanks," Jacob replied. "This time I think I'm gonna need it."

Chapter Thirteen

AFTER JACOB HAD taken Anna and started to head back to Rockliffe Manor, cushioned by her eternal gratitude and a million expressions of it, Batya started to pace the floor of the living room. She needed to figure out what kind of rabbit she could pull out of a hat if Jacob didn't deliver.

Her phone buzzed. She stood, crossed the room, and picked it up from on top of the coffee table where she'd left it.

The text was from Abe.

A: We don't have much time. You want I should pick you up?

Usually a random text from Abe would get her excited, joyous. But this one made her nervous.

B: I'm not sure what you're talking about.

She stared at the phone, watching the dots move in sync as he either thought or typed.

A: Consider this me calling you. You texted me.

B: Yeah. To tell you that I lost my lecturer for next

week.

A: For meat, right?

B: Yeah. For meat. I accepted a friend's offer of help. So maybe he has someone already.

A: I know. I was there when Jacob got the call. I was going to call you anyway, but telling you now I was with him when his fiancée called saves us trouble later.

Which was nice. Really nice.

A: But either way, because I thought about it and because you're important, I want to take you to meet a friend of mine.

She was not going to spend hours pondering what he meant by "important." Instead she focused on the other part, the one that was slightly less fraught.

B: Friend? I am intrigued.

A: He is Shomer Shabbas, so if we really want to chat with him, we have like no time. I had to beg and plead with him to wait for us.

She paused, watching the dots move. A useful friend who was Sabbath observant. Very interesting. And if nothing else, she was fascinated by the idea.

Who could it be?

No matter. She was ready to take him up on his offer.

B: How long do I have?

A: Ten minutes. If you need more, let me know.

Ten minutes. Ten minutes would be enough time to get herself ready. She could only hope whoever it was could save her and the class from certain doom.

❯❯❯❮❮❮

ABE PULLED UP to Batya's house, his heart pounding in his chest. As he reached for his phone to call and tell her he'd arrived, he heard a knock on the window.

"Come on in," he said as he hit the unlock button.

She was stunning. Gorgeous for sure, but the way the setting sun hit the color in her brown hair was magic.

"So we're going adventuring," she said, her voice blowing through his thoughts.

"Adventuring," he replied with a laugh as he pulled out, down the street toward the center of town.

"To destinations known or unknown?"

He paused for a second, enjoying the tone of her voice. "I don't know if you've been there before, but you've definitely seen his place."

"A he, huh?"

"Yep. A he."

"And you think," she continued, attempting to play detective, "he's useful?"

"Generally," he replied, giving her something he knew she'd jump right on. "But, specifically to you, definitely

145

useful."

She raised an eyebrow. "Why would he be specifically useful to me?"

"You'll know when we get there," he said, wanting to give her some kind of fun of discovery.

"Why are we playing twenty questions?"

"Because you like to solve mysteries, right?"

She paused, and he watched the thoughts run across her face. "I guess?"

"And I figure you're probably stressed about a billion things."

"So you'd give me another thing to stress about?"

He sighed, turning down the familiar street and in to the parking lot. "I didn't mean to be stress inducing. I thought it would be fun. Give your brain something else to focus on. I'm sorry if I stressed you out further."

She didn't say anything, and as he searched for a parking space close to the shop, he wondered if he'd lost her. "Do you want me to take you home?"

She shook her head. "No. It's fine. I know you're trying to be helpful. I know you're sticking your neck out for me here." She paused. "I didn't miss the fact that you're trying to get me here before your friend leaves for the night."

He smiled as he pulled into the spot of his dreams. "He's got really short hours on Friday so he can get home and ready before sundown, so it's always better to catch him before he leaves on Thursday night. Anyway, I tried not to make it too obvious."

"Makes sense. But you failed, miserably."

He smiled again, back at her. "We're here. You ready to meet my very useful friend?"

Her answering smile was a work of art. "Yes," she said. "Let's do this."

He didn't take her hand, but he moved to the other side to open the door.

"Follow me," he said with a grin of his own as they headed up the stairs to the set of stores.

"Can I guess by process of elimination?"

"No," he said. "You really don't want to spoil the surprise."

Which is what he said, even though it wasn't much of a surprise.

But there was laughter in her eyes now. Even as they made it to the top of the stairs, and turned right toward the set of stores he spent most of his shopping time in. The gourmet store, and right next to it was…

"You brought me to a butcher?"

He beamed. "Not just any butcher," he replied. "My butcher. The one who gives me good, kosher meat. Who is a third-generation butcher in Rivertown. He's waiting for us."

And as he watched her compose herself, pull back the emotions that were riding below the surface, he nodded.

BATYA STOOD THERE, wide-eyed as Abe opened the door to the shop. It was out of a storybook, if the storybook was set in Eastern Europe at the turn of the century.

The lighting was bright, as if it were brand new, but the photographs on the brick walls were sepia-toned, so the place had been around for a while. Hebrew letters spelling Yiddish words were painted onto the tile just below the crown moldings.

Kosher.

Fleishig.

The shelves were stocked and clean, the products in boxes and bags labeled with familiar last names, reminding her of days of religious school treats and time spent with her grandparents.

It smelled clean, of lemon and hours spent attempting to clear off the scent of freshly cut meat, done by someone who cared about the place and their customers.

"*Nu?*" Abe called out.

Yiddish, huh? Which meant the person they were meeting understood the word – a combination of what's going on and where are you at the same time. Curiouser and curiouser.

"Aaaabe. You're here. My wife was starting to text me, wondering if she should lock the door."

The voice was slightly accented, and she met a pair of twinkling brown eyes.

"And who is this that you've brought to meet me?"

"This," Abe said, "is Batya. She and I have known each other for a long time."

"Batya, hmm. An interesting name."

"If it helps make it less interesting, my last name is Averman," she replied. "So, I come by it and my curiosity honestly. Speaking of curiosity, who are you?"

The man smiled. "Moshe Geirowitz. Moshe the butcher, son of my father, recently retired to Florida."

"So many snowbirds," she replied with a smile of her own. "Mine are there too. I think in Aventura?"

Moshe waved a hand. "Boca maybe. They're not here, and life is good for them wherever they are. But you?"

"She has questions about kosher meat," Abe interjected. "And maybe—"

"What he means is," she said with a smile, "I'd like to learn about kosher butchering, and possibly maybe ask you to potentially teach a class on Wednesday."

"A class for the fakakta latke competition?" Moshe turned to Abe. "Is this why you wanted to bring her to ask me?"

"What I'd really love," she said, trying to keep from getting nervous, "if nothing else, is a conversation and maybe something for my website. Because I want to learn, and if Abe trusts you, I do too."

"You should watch some of her interviews. They're fantastic," Abe interjected. "And the class that was aired the second week, the one with the history of Jewish food lecture?

That was phenomenal."

"Wait." Moshe tapped a finger on the counter. "Was that the show with the conversation about spice?"

Batya nodded. "Yes. That was."

"So like a talk about butchering for aspiring kosher chefs, hmm? Is that what you want?"

Batya nodded. "On a Wednesday night. Possibly."

"Next Wednesday night," Abe clarified.

"And," she added, "if not that, maybe we can have a conversation on another day?"

There was a moment where the look in Moshe's eyes made her feel as if she'd made the worst decision. But Abe was steady, and she was glad she could notice that through the haze of her zombie crush.

"Hokay," Moshe said finally, nodding. "You do this thing, for…for what?"

"Because," she said, once she'd figured out the words she needed, "I want to tell the stories of Jewish food on television."

"Well," Moshe replied, "if this fakakta latke competition brings his food to the world, and gives you this shot…" he paused "…I think it's a good thing. So sign me up."

No matter how excited she was, kissing Abe right now would be a horrible idea.

And if she said it enough times, she would actually start to believe it.

Chapter Fourteen

FRIDAY WAS SLOW, and as sundown came around, Abe was fighting with dough.

Not a challah dough; that had long been dealt with and was sitting on the cutting board, ready for dinner.

The results of this dough were sinking into the pot instead of floating. He wasn't getting the proportions right, and the dough had gone to garbage.

Thankfully, hopefully, his dinner guest wouldn't care too much about whether his matzah balls were fluffy.

"What are you making and why are you cooking already?"

Abe looked up from the stove, only to see Artur standing behind him. "Oh," he said with a laugh. "It's you."

"*Shabbat shalom* to you too," his friend said. "And what the heck are you making and why can't I pour sour cream over it?"

"Why in the world would you want to pour sour cream over matzah balls?"

"That's something even I wouldn't condone. Not even matzah balls that don't seem to float." He paused. "What did you use? Water?"

Abe nodded. "Can't get the proportions right."

"Seltzer," he said. "My mother used to swear on the rising properties of seltzer, before she decided that cooking was something other people did."

And as Abe pondered that little bit of information, his friend stared deeper into the pot.

"So, chicken soup?"

Abe nodded. "I got some extra chicken last night from Moshe, so I made soup. You're welcome."

"Well of course. I get the benefit of your extra chicken since—wait." He paused. "Last night?"

"Yeah. Took Batya to see him last night."

Artur nodded, pulled open a drawer, and started to take out some silverware. "Okay. I'm listening."

"That assumes I'm telling you this wild story."

"It does indeed, but of course what would our *chatzi Shabbas* dinner be without wild stories, hmm?"

Which was true, of course. Nights with Leo meant cooking and humor. Nights with Artur meant food and stories, sometimes hard ones, sometimes easy ones.

And there was some degree of solemnity of a Friday night with challah and wine and candles, of remembrance if not exactly observance. And so, as they sat down to eat not long after, Abe told Artur the story.

"Interesting," Artur said as he took a drink of his soda. "So you mean to tell me that you brought her to Moshe and she hasn't told you whether she's coming tomorrow morning?"

Abe nodded. "That about sums it up, I think."

"It's safe to say she'll be here tomorrow morning. Or afternoon or sometime tomorrow. I mean, you basically showed her your etchings."

Abe barely kept from covering Artur with the soup in his mouth. "What do etchings have to do with Moshe the butcher?"

Artur sighed. Which usually meant some kind of pronouncement was coming. "I think what you did is showed her your ace in the hole, the most important thing to your setup. Which is basically etchings to the two of you. The forbidden, the 'let me show you this' but what I mean is 'let me show you myself.'"

"I still don't get it."

"You gave her something not very many people know about you. For instance, I don't know Moshe. I didn't know he existed."

"Do you actually go food shopping in Rivertown aside from at my house?"

Artur snickered. "Yes. I know where the kosher butcher place is, next to that way too expensive gourmet store you like, the one that claims it makes blintzes."

Of course, with Artur, everything came down to blintzes.

"But," his friend continued. "I don't know it like you do. I don't know the guy who gives you his consistently best meat, and unapologetically stans your barbecue, or whatever they're calling it these days. You're showing Batya your secrets, and it means something to her, or at least it should."

Which meant he shouldn't have been surprised by the late-night knock at his door, heralding a package from the food delivery company that had brought her first response gift.

He opened the door and took a bag from the driver's outstretched hands. He couldn't help himself, and immediately read the attached card as soon as he saw it, even before he went back inside.

Abe,

Late night sweets that will be fuel for tomorrow. Looking forward to seeing you.

Batya

He opened the package only to discover coconut macaroons, dipped in chocolate. Three different kinds.

His favorite.

He couldn't wait to see her.

THE NEXT MORNING, Batya wondered why she'd sent Abe macaroons as a way of announcing she'd be taking him up on his offer of a visit.

Yes, Anna joked that Jacob was her hamantaschen, but

they didn't need a reason to make anything a private joke; she'd argue that they'd need a reason to not turn a random *thing* into a joke between them. And Sarah, at all times, needled Isaac about being her rugelach, which thankfully made Isaac smile.

Anna said that Jacob had the hard shell with the visible jelly center to anybody who actually paid attention. And Sarah was convinced that Isaac was both softer and harder than he appeared, just like the rugelach.

But they were in relationships with the objects of their pastry-filled desires.

Batya just had a crush, some history, and a bridge.

She couldn't explain to anybody that Abe was soft and could be molded and yet he was perseverant. Macaroons were persistent little pastries who held their shape no matter what life, and cooking, threw at them. They were derided, "improved" and consistently ignored. But they persevered, and they deserved to be celebrated.

Just like Abe.

And if she was going to be honest with herself, she wanted to spend time with him. Not in the "indulging the revitalized crush" sort of way but the sharing thoughts over food ways, like they'd been doing. Which sent her to his house the next afternoon, bearing a large thermos.

"It's good to see you," he said. "I'm glad you came."

"I come bearing tea," she said with a smile.

"You brought me tea?" he asked, as he ushered her inside. "You sent me macaroons, which I loved, but you don't have to send me anything else."

"There are," Batya began, completely nonplussed by his confusing greeting as she stepped through the door, "many ways of making tea and many different ways of drinking it. The most underappreciated by most people on the East Coast, and the best to match with barbecue, is sweet tea. Proportions vary according to recipe, and I figured I'd bring you my favorite."

"I appreciate it," he said with a smile. "I mean it's not necessary that you bring me anything else, but I really appreciate it."

And oh, that smile. She felt it all the way down to her toes. "You stuck out your neck for me on Thursday," she said, trying to shove her brain back into the moment. "The least I could do is this."

"Looking forward to trying it," he said with a smile.

This one was different though, there was something about it that…

Nope. She wasn't doing that again. She wasn't analyzing him, wasn't shoving every single part of their interactions under a microscope.

"You okay?"

She nodded. "Fine," she said. "I have my phone if I want to record things for the blog."

"Great," he said. "I didn't think of that, but sure. Whatever helps make you comfortable works for me."

"What did you think this was going to be, and why do you think I'm uncomfortable?"

She couldn't help but notice how long it took him to answer, and when she was just about to fill the space with words, he smiled.

"There are a lot of times where we're uncomfortable," he finally said. "I didn't think this was going to be an interview, but if you want it to be, that's totally fine. I just wanted to share this with you because I figure you'd appreciate it, you know?"

Batya nodded, and once again, letting herself fall into the moment and the emotions that were bubbling just beneath the surface, was dangerous. Treating this like a business, as if she were doing an onsite interview for FoodWorld would be safer. "You do this yourself?"

"I do," Abe said after a bit of time where she was ignoring the confusion in his eyes. "I do most of it by myself, and then because I realized I was becoming a social outcast, I invite someone over to keep me company each week, to help or whatever they feel comfortable doing, whether it's just somehow helping me to fill the orders, or cleaning the pellet grill if I use it, and anything and more in between. It's much more fun this way. And easier later when we're fulfilling the orders."

"I see." So she actually was here to help him, to learn how he did pop-up barbecue from his backyard. Which meant she'd spend the afternoon covered in his custom barbecue sauce, all the way up to her elbows.

She couldn't wait.

"Thank you."

He smiled. "You're welcome."

And just when she was about to ask him how his barbecue journey started, her stomach made its opinion known.

"You said you'd feed me."

Abe smiled. "I did, didn't I?" He gestured toward the table and the spread he'd laid out.

Tradition. Of course.

Bagels, lox, whitefish, cream cheese, and all the things they wouldn't be able to touch when they were actually working with the meat. And coffee seemingly strong enough to burn the insides of her nose.

"This," Batya said, swiping a plain bagel from the plate and picking up a knife to cut it in half, "is amazing." She paused, and debated whether to use the scallion or the plain cream cheese. "Baum's or Caf and Nosh?"

Abe laughed as he spread cream cheese on his bagel. "Where else but Baum's in this town?"

Batya shook her head. "Too true," she said with a laugh. "Anything going on with Baum's?"

"Don't think so," he said. "Not since we were there a few weeks ago. They've got good bagels but still have ridiculous Saturday morning lines."

"Before shul?" The question came out without thinking; she hadn't been to the Rivertown Synagogue in a long time and hadn't thought about it in even longer. And yet the familiar Yiddish term everybody who went there used for it was a reflex.

Abe nodded as if she hadn't said anything earth-shattering or difficult. "Yeah. Right before shul, everyone wants a bagel."

"Everybody just wants a bagel."

He laughed, and this easy, comfortable banter on a Saturday was, oddly enough, what she'd wanted from him, what she'd always hoped they'd have. An easy, companionable situation where they'd enjoy the seconds turning into minutes, the conversation flowing like Niagara Falls and…

No.

Hoping for anything with Abe was dangerous. Bad. It led her places she didn't want to go, to thoughts she'd spent way too much of her life attempting to shut down. She was not going to spend her Saturday fanning the flames of emotions that deserved to be buried.

Futile emotions were exhausting, and she'd vowed years ago that she wasn't engaging in speculative romance.

And this easy banter, as if she and Abe were friends without baggage or history, was great. But acting as if he was her end goal or the perfection she needed in her life wasn't good for her or for them.

Which left her only one alternative.

She changed the subject.

ABE DIDN'T KNOW what had happened.

For the first time in his life, things with Batya were actually going smoothly. They were bantering over bagels and whitefish, and then she'd clammed up.

Completely.

Had he done something? Said something? Was it the conversation about the shul?

Because if he was going to be honest with himself, that was where it got weird. It had taken much longer than usual for her to reply, which should have signified trouble.

But he hadn't noticed. Not really.

He shouldn't have answered. He should have deflected or made some ridiculous joke about the stunt the head of the local branch of Baum's had pulled. Anything that would have kept their train from derailing off the happy track.

Now he had to take action. But how?

Maybe he should start with an apology.

"Look," he said as he started to clean up the dishes, "I don't know what—"

"It's fine," she said. "I'm a bit at loose ends. It's not you."

"Fair enough." He didn't want to push it; he was glad she was giving him that much.

Batya turned toward the window and what seemed to him like the rest of the dishes at the table. "You wash, and if you give me towels, I'll dry."

A reprieve. "Nice change of subject," he said, with a smile that was hopefully nonchalant, "but it's an offer I will accept."

She didn't say anything when he opened a drawer and unearthed a bunch of dish towels. "Here," he said, offering them to her. "If you really want to do this."

"You don't have a dishwasher," she said. "I kinda have no choice."

He laughed. "You're throwing yourself down on the sword of hospitality for no reason."

"What do you mean?"

This was the big one, and he'd rather make it clear from the beginning that he understood what was going on. "The truth is, I do have a dishwasher," he said, opening the cabinet to the left of the sink and pointing to the dishwasher he'd had installed. "Honestly? Doing barbecue on the weekends without a dishwasher would be the worst kind of torture."

She raised an eyebrow in a way that signaled she was going to take the bait. "So why did you head to the sink? Are you the kind who ignores all the wisdom about how silly it is to pre-rinse your dishes?"

He laughed; he loved bantering with her. Adored it. Even about dishes. "Well," he said, "I have to clean up somehow, and you looked like you needed to take a break from conversation. Doing dishes is a good way to do that. At least I think so."

She blew out a breath before taking the pack of dish towels he offered her. They worked in silence, him washing, her drying, until she looked up and turned toward him. "I'm struggling with the spaces in between what we say to each other."

"So do you want more conversation or less?" he asked. "I'm confused."

She smiled, and this one was a bit better. "I am too. I think it might be better if we talk more, you know? But like, carefully."

He nodded. Talking to her was fun, easy. "So what's off limits then?"

"That's…" She paused. "I don't know."

He did, but he wasn't going to start talking about the graduation party or her sudden departure from Rivertown just yet. Especially considering she needed to set the rules. She needed to be comfortable.

"Until we figure out what our rhythm is, maybe you can tell me about barbecue. Why you started."

"Common ground, then? Food ground?"

She nodded, and he could see the tension ease from her shoulders. "Yes. That. Because it seems like a place I like to stay with you." And then, as if she'd said too much, she focused on the drying.

That was fine. He put the newly cleaned plate down on the rack before stepping back. "Okay," he said, reaching for the cookbook, the one his father had given to him as he headed to college. "My barbecue story starts here. With this."

And as he told Batya the story about how a homesick college kid in the middle of upstate New York made friends using the tools he'd been given, he hoped she'd understand that he was using those same tools to try and make amends.

SPENDING THIS DAY with Abe had been…

A choice.

She hadn't quite decided whether it had been a good choice or a bad one; that was definitely still up in the air. But she was learning about him, learning about his journey along with his barbecue. Trying to see the man he'd become.

The one who turned homesick weekends spent cooking in dorm kitchens in Binghamton, into something that would define most of his adult life, through college and then business school in Massachusetts.

He was now, even more so, someone she admired.

Not to mention, she was desperately trying not to fall in love with him again. Because the pounds of tension she was ignoring pulled at the two of them. That kind of energy was going to choke her in the end.

As opposed to the actual, tangible smoke, the hickory and cherry flavors emanating from his smoker and the gorgeous bricking on the meat it had produced. Anybody who said beef was boring was lying or deluded or both.

She'd label them wrong.

"You," she said as he'd cut another piece of meat, "are really good at this."

Thankfully, she was wielding two forks, forcing herself to focus on separating the super tender beef into orders for those who wanted it pulled.

"Thanks," he said. "I'm glad you think so." He paused and looked at her.

What the heck was going on?

She was trying not to analyze him or his expressions, but the fact was that she couldn't help but try to get behind the scenes of the one he had on his face.

If she was allowing herself a bit of speculation, she'd say he looked like he was watching lightning in a bottle. But still.

It felt weird.

"Have I covered my face in barbecue sauce, or is there something important you'd like to say to me?" She paused before she managed to say something really, really unwise. "Keep in mind that I'm wielding two forks at the moment."

"I was just going to ask if you liked what you tried last weekend."

Why did he sound so casual?

Maybe he was trying to hide how nervous he was about hearing her opinion of his barbecue. Did her opinion matter that much to him?

"Well," she finally said. She wanted to be as clear as she could, give him the kind of praise that would make him happy as a chef. "I like the rub, and I liked the sauce."

"Thank you," he said.

She smiled back at him. And then it was her turn. "Speaking of thank-yous, I wanted to thank you for the saves, you know for the class and for the lecture."

He smiled easily. "Think nothing of it, really. You needed me, and I, you know, was there."

Which was something she didn't really want to contemplate, how easy it was for him to jump in and save her. He'd done it a few times already, and thinking about it was starting to make her feel things she didn't want to acknowledge. "I really appreciate it," she said. "You've done it so easily and I just…"

"You just what?"

"I'm just glad you're there," she said, forcing the conversation and the subject to a halt. The last thing she needed was to explore how she felt about him always being there to save her. "Anyway," she continued, searching for something to say that didn't have anything to do with rescues or damsels. "I'm excited to see what tonight's going to be."

"Me too. I'm enjoying spending time with you, and showing you this part of my life."

She smiled, but she didn't say much. Because anything else would send her directly towards emotional speculation. And nothing good could come of it. Hope in believing and following a crush that should have died years ago wasn't doing anybody any favors. Especially her.

ABE WAS TOO confused for words. He was off balance and entirely too unsure of what was going on. Being around Batya was like being on a tempest-tossed ship.

But this was not the time to think or analyze. This was the time where he needed her help, and the orders were coming in fast.

"You ready?" he asked.

She turned to his whiteboard, the chart, and the descriptions; they'd gone over everything a few times by this point, and they were getting close to go time.

"Yep," she said. "At least I think so."

And as the clock turned over, the most important part of the night had begun. There was no pausing, no thinking, just rapid motion. Her muscles moved fluidly, organizing orders as she went, passing him bags and containers. He'd shout out the number, and she'd pass the ready made containers over. Containers in hand, he'd run outside only to come back with another number and start the process again.

Working with her felt like a well-oiled machine. Smooth like silk or margarine or vegan butter or any of those illusions writers made to soft, easygoing things. But parve. Safe for serving with meat. It was as if they'd been made to work together, even more fluid than working with Artur. But the thing about working with Batya was that as the night went on, he got to watch her confidence bloom out of her in ways he'd never seen before.

And by the end of the night, after the dishwasher had been filled a few times, the smoker had been taken care of, and the pellet grill had been cleaned, they'd earned the dinner he'd prepared. There was brisket he'd saved for them, with a few of the sides: tater tots and the special applesauce he'd made just for them.

He poured her sweet tea into mason jars, and it was a perfect cap to the night.

"This was amazing," he said as he walked her to the front door. "Special. Thank you."

His hand brushed against hers, the electricity moving up his skin.

But he didn't pull away, not like before. Not like he had for years. He wasn't afraid of this moment.

She leaned in closer; he could smell the sweet tea and the barbecue sauce on her breath. It smelled exquisite, familiar, like she was wearing perfume he'd made for her. But this wasn't flowers or scents meant only to be smelled. This was meant to be tasted.

"Can I?" he asked.

"Can you what?"

"You have a bit of sauce. May I remove it?"

"That depends on where."

Carefully, he leaned closer, her breath intoxicating him, and brushed a finger across her lower lip to remove the sauce that beckoned him closer.

"May I kiss you?"

"Yes," she said.

But then she looked away from him. She was nervous; he'd seen her nervous for years, and he recognized the signs pouring out of her now.

"I don't know why you'd want to, but yes." Batya was trying to be nonchalant, but he'd spent his life watching her. She wasn't nonchalant about this.

He wasn't either. Which is why he had to make it clear how much kissing her meant to him. "I do," he said. "I absolutely, one hundred percent, do."

"Kiss me, then," she said.

He slowly felt his way towards her, leaning the rest of the way in. Watching the moods change in her eyes as he brushed her lips with his, the softest and lightest touch at first. But the taste of her pulled him in like a tractor beam, filled him with desire.

Her tongue joined his in a dance that made him giddy, made him wonder what the hell he'd been thinking for all those years. He'd lost so many years of this kiss, so many years of discovering her lips, and her. But now that he knew what kissing Batya felt like, Abe wanted to spend the rest of his life feeling like this, kissing her, discovering her moods and her smiles.

Suddenly she was gone, the November cold strong on his lips. And when he met her eyes, the ice he saw there broke him.

"What. The. Hell?" she asked.

His brain stopped, shuddered.

What had happened? What was going on? What did he do? Words tossed and turned, tripping over each other as he desperately tried to figure out what he was going to say. "I—"

"I can't do this. It's too much. We can't do this."

"Batya, please—"

"No," she said, her very clear and final words broke the tension between them completely and utterly, leaving desolation in its wake. It was tangible, and it *hurt*.

So this is what it felt like. This is what a taste of possibility, of optimism that exploded felt like. "Batya."

"I can't do this. I can't do this."

Without letting him reply, respond, answer, anything, she headed past him, down the walkway, leaving him behind.

He'd lived in this place mostly by himself for the last three years, but he'd never felt so alone before.

Chapter Fifteen

ON SUNDAY MORNING, Batya's emotions were all over the place, which meant she needed help.

An expert.

And she knew just the person to ask.

Just three years before, Anna had proclaimed her history with Jacob was radioactive baggage. Now she was six months away from marrying him. If anybody could help her figure out how she wanted to handle things with Abe, it was Anna.

Thankfully for her, Anna was in Hollowville with Jacob, and agreed to meet her at the Caf and Nosh.

She left earlier than usual, found a spot by Tante Shelly's apartment, and meandered down the street, resolving to stop by and see her aunt before heading back to Rivertown.

The cold had seemingly ushered the early stirrings of Hanukkah into Hollowville. But the most important things would never change. The smell of the Caf and Nosh as she walked inside, the feeling she got from walking into a place that knew her as well as she knew it.

And the embrace of a friend who'd seen her through some interesting times. Instead of waiting for her to approach, Anna crossed the threshold and put her arms around her.

"I missed you," Batya said. "I missed this."

"Me too," her friend said.

But after a bit, Anna stepped back. "So, what's up?"

"I need advice," she said as Anna ushered her through the entrance, past the front desk, following Chana's finger to an open table.

"Talk to me. What's going on? I've honestly had enough looking at real estate."

"Real estate?" Adult relationships apparently required discussions on real estate. Houses, apartments, condos. Especially if this was an adult relationship like the one Anna was in.

"Yeah," Anna said as they sat down. "Something small, I told him. *Small.* So, we're looking at houses because my parents aren't getting younger, and at some point he thinks we're going to need something here. And, apparently, because he's right, that *sometime* is now."

"So," Chana interjected as she came over to the table, dropping off menus as if they needed them. "Are you okay?"

The thing still hanging over her from last class. Not the missing instructor, but the panic attack she'd had all the way through the beginning of it. She hadn't expected Chana to mention it. "Fine," she said. "Thank you. Really."

Chana nodded, though Batya could still see the skepticism in the older woman's eyes. "You ready to order?"

STACEY AGDERN

Grateful for the break, Batya threw herself into ordering, with coffee and matzah brei and all of the best breakfast foods.

And as Chana headed off to the kitchen, Anna raised an eyebrow.

"You're doing okay though?"

Batya nodded. "With that, yeah. You were sweet on Thursday."

"I'm your friend," Anna replied. "This is how things go. When you call me and tell me you're upset, and I just happen to be on my way to Hollowville, I end up at your place instead."

"That's not what I meant, but thank you. Always. But I have a question for you."

Anna nodded. "Okay."

"How do you trust your feelings?"

Anna looked up at her. "What do you mean exactly?"

"Well, how do you tell the difference between feelings that are resonant, ones that are remnants of old ties, and something genuine, something new? If anybody could help me figure out how to get out of my head and trust my emotions, it would be my friend who's engaged to her childhood sweetheart."

Anna put her hand on hers. "I'm guessing you're talking about Abe? The guy who made you spill tea?"

She nodded. "Yeah. Him. The object of my unrequited high school crush turned…whoever he is."

"So here's what you need to remember," Anna said, as if she was making a point she'd made many times before. "I'm not engaged to my childhood sweetheart, and dear God, I hate when people say that. Some people can say that. But not me."

Batya raised an eyebrow. "I'm not following."

Anna lay back against the cushioned bench.

"I'm engaged to the man my childhood sweetheart has *become*. If I were engaged to my childhood sweetheart, things would have gone downhill really quickly."

"So tell me. What's the difference, because I am all ears," Batya said.

"You're going to have to lock seventeen-year-old Batya out of the room and out of your decisions."

"I don't get it."

"Seventeen-year-old Batya had hopes and dreams and a ton of disappointments. All of them drove you to become who you are now. Who, as far as I'm concerned, is a darn good person," Anna said with a smile.

"Thank you?"

"But here's the deal, and this is important. Your history with Abe and your Rivertown friends can help to illuminate your relationship with any and all of them now. It *cannot* define those relationships."

Batya took a drink of her water. "Right. That's the resonance question. The resonance I have is made up of feelings seventeen-year-old Batya had and, truth to tell, that resonance is the reason I'm having trouble trusting my feelings, whatever they are, when I'm with Abe now."

"Right." Anna took a sip of her coffee and Batya could tell her friend was trying to be as specific and clear as she could be. "For Jacob and I, the resonance is our history—it's baggage, shared experiences, and dirty laundry; our name for them changes at any given moment. But, dear God, we'd be, and in fact were, in trouble as long as we let any of those things define us. Yes, there are a lifetime of inside jokes we yank out from time to time. But that's *all they are*. And, more importantly, all they should be."

"You mean," Batya said, "they're footnotes to the conversation, not the main conversation."

"Exactly. And for us, they're all based on real, lived experiences, not seen through the lens of an insidious crush that spent more than fifteen years eating you up alive."

"So what does this mean for me, Anna. Please," she said. "Talk to me like I'm five. What do I do? How do I deal with this?"

Anna sighed, as if her point was either as clear as she could make it or something she had trouble getting herself. "Ask yourself some basic questions. Is he a good person?"

Was Abe a good person now?

He'd taken over the house he'd grown up in, made barbecue on the weekends, had a day job he was good at, and was a nice guy to his friends and his father. And he'd been nice with her recently. "Yes. He came to my aid when I needed him in the class and the audition."

Anna nodded. "Good. I like that answer. Is he someone you could easily be with now?"

"I don't know. Because easy is lovely with him, easy is fun with him, but I'm always questioning—"

"No, stop right there," Anna said before she took another sip of her coffee. "The second you start to question your instincts here is when seventeen-year-old Batya comes in to make things difficult. Trust me, I know about annoying seventeen-year-olds and their interference. So I'm asking again. Is he someone you could easily be with now?"

"I don't know."

Anna nodded. "Okay. Maybe an easier question. Is he someone you *want* to be with now?"

There was a problem, a rather large obstacle in the way. "We don't communicate," she said.

"I hate to tell you, but that doesn't matter right now. Communication is especially hard when one of you is acting based on fifteen-year-old information and the other one is acting on the cutting edge of innovative technology. And no, I'm not telling you which is which."

Batya snorted as Anna took a sip of her coffee.

"Communication," her friend continued, "as I also know, can be easily fixed if both of you understand there *is* a problem. So. Again, we go back to that question. What does the Batya of today think of the Abe of today?"

But was he, insidious zombie crush aside, for *her*? "I

think he's a nice guy, a good guy."

"Anything else?"

"I don't know," Batya admitted. "I really don't know."

"And that is where you have to start," Anna said as Chana brought their food. "Whatever happens between you two needs to start *now*, based on what you know of each other *now*. What he makes you feel like *now*."

Batya decided that was very good and clear advice she could follow. She had to ignore the cheering section, ignore the peanut gallery, and figure out her own heart.

No matter what decision it made.

ABE COULDN'T CONCENTRATE and his brain was firing a mile a minute. There were also tons of loads of laundry he'd been neglecting and a bathroom that...well, needed attention.

So instead, he spent Sunday listening to music, podcasts, and an Empires game, and cleaned the house from top to bottom. But by dinnertime, the house was sparkling, the laundry was done, and he still hadn't slowed down. The replay of the scene from the night before was stronger not weaker.

He needed to figure out how to deal with what was bothering him. He decided to test a new recipe and called Artur. Thankfully, his friend was free and offered to bring drinks.

When Artur arrived, he took a long sniff of the kitchen and smiled. "I'm glad you're prepping for the fry-off, but this isn't exactly the kind of thing I expected."

"I'm feeding you," Abe replied with a laugh. "And you are my favorite latke tester."

"Bonded by Hebrew school," Artur said with a nod, clearly reflecting on their shared history as Abe had intended. "And again, snot-nosed kids. So. What happened?"

And because the latkes were frying, the homemade applesauce smelled better than he'd expected, and because Artur knew him way too well, Abe launched into the tale of Saturday night's disaster, ending with, "I kissed her. Which was the worst idea of all."

Artur sat against the chair, and like he had on so many late nights they'd spent talking about random nonsense, mulled over the situation. "I don't know if it's a bad thing you kissed her."

"You don't know?" He paced, paused, and then stopped just to glare at his friend, as if the answer was obvious. "Of course it's bad."

"It's a bad idea you kissed her without talking to her."

Nothing with Batya was easy, especially if it involved him and emotions he hadn't even managed to confess to himself. "How can I talk to her if it always ends up in havoc?"

Artur sighed, shook his head, a clear sign that some kind

of pronouncement was on its way. "It always ends up in havoc because you haven't figured out how to navigate chaos."

"This isn't a time to be obscure or pithy or whatever." He was feeling weird, made of angles underneath his skin, dynamite exploding at any wrong spot. "I'm sorry."

But this was old hat for both of them; sometimes he was giving pronouncements and Artur was staring listlessly into a plate of pierogis, and sometimes, like now, Abe was at the stove, trying to smooth off his edges.

"So," Artur finally said. "Chaos, perspective. You don't have it. The moment that shaped her life, was, unfortunate-ly, a blip on yours. A painful blip when you remember, but let's face it, a blip. And where you see a blip, she sees a boulder. It's a great optical illusion, right? But a really horrible way of seeing and continuing a relationship between two people."

A map led to one single point. One important point. A graduation party and an eighteen-year-old drinking a beer he clearly should not have. "Which is why it's bad I kissed her." Abe said, flipping the last batch and taking them out of the pan.

He watched, his plate full of steaming latkes, as his friend folded his arms. "Did you even ask her or did you plunder her lips like a pirate?"

For a second, Abe had some random image in his head of a treasure map and a spot marked X.

He yanked his brain out of the weird place and tried not to laugh. "I don't know what that even is," he told his friend as he put the plate down on the table. "But no, I asked her if I could kiss her. She said yes. And, fireworks."

"And did you immediately say how amazing it was, and that you wanted to spend the rest of your life with her?"

"No."

That he was sure of, as was the relief on Artur's face.

"Did you look like you could see the stars and the secret of the universe in her eyes?"

That, unfortunately he didn't know. There had been earth-shattering thoughts in his brain, and it wasn't as if he'd actually said any of them aloud. He hoped.

Dear God.

He knew Batya had broken the kiss, and the look on her face haunted him. But what was it? What had turned the yes to horror?

Had he spoken? Had he said some random nonsense that scared her? Had he managed to break the moment entirely on his own?

"I'm not sure," he admitted. "I don't know."

"Yeah," Artur said. "That explains it. You have no poker face with this woman, and until you and she can figure out how to communicate in the chaos, you need to learn one."

"I'm hopeless," Abe decided, running a hand through his hair. "Really and completely hopeless."

Artur shook his head. "You're not hopeless. All you have

to do is learn how to wield a stick of dynamite."

Abe found himself laughing. "I have no idea what you're talking about, but sure."

"Seriously," Artur said as he speared a latke from the plate. "You need a poker face, and it's been too long since I've played. Who else do you know who plays? Because none of the people in our group can play worth anything, and you need someone who knows to teach you."

"I might know someone," he said, thinking of the conversation he'd had at Leo's. "But you have to promise me we play for peanuts. Literally. No money, no favors, no nothing. Peanuts or chocolate chips or Chanukah gelt."

"What is this? I play for paper clips."

Abe nodded. "Okay. That's fine. We play for paper clips. And maybe slip in a dreidel or two."

"That sounds fun. I'm now curious, by the way. Who's joining us that you don't want to play with anything of value?"

"A friend," he said. "Money is pressure, favors are worse, unless we were snot-nosed kids together."

"You called him," Artur beamed. "You called him. And you don't want pressure. That's fine. Making friends as an adult is fakakta anyway, and so less pressure when you're learning a poker face."

The way Artur's mind worked was dizzying most of the time, and so, per usual, Abe nodded. "Yes. You were right and yes."

"I will take my praise in latkes, and maybe some sour cream?"

"Stop with the s-word or I won't take out some of the leftovers I was going to feed you."

"That is rude, my friend. Absolutely rude. Fine. I will try your homemade applesauce under protest. But I will not forget the threat."

And as Abe snickered, organizing the things he needed to, he texted Jacob and started to plan a poker night.

>>>><<<<

ABE DISCOVERED THAT wanting a poker night and actually planning it were two different things. There were many dynamics and variables and things to make sure he had. Cards and the paper clips, as well as the chocolate gelt of course. And then the food. Basics. Beer, cream soda, pierogis, blintzes, and knishes. Finger food. Dairy.

He was cooking when the bell rang. "Door's open," he yelled.

"You sure?"

Of course, it was Jacob who arrived first, because Artur was never, ever early or on time. "Yep. I'm at the stove, so come on in."

A few minutes later, he heard footsteps and Jacob entered the kitchen. "Nice place," he said.

"Grew up here," Abe replied with a smile. "Glad you

could make it."

"Good to be here." And then a pause. "Wednesday's class is going to be at the same place Anna's was? At the high school?"

Abe nodded as he watched the stove. "Yep. That's the plan as far as I know. And I got someone to help, so if you didn't manage to convince whoever you needed to, it's okay."

Jacob shook his head. "Thanks for thinking of that, but no. It'll be good that my contact is not speaking alone."

"No. He won't be alone." Abe smiled. And, oddly enough, that was the gist of it. That was what the problem was. "Just keep me posted, about anything really. If he balks at the last minute, if you get stuck on the expressway, or if any number of random extra things happen between now and Wednesday night."

"Thank you."

Abe raised an eyebrow. "For what?"

"It's hard for me to admit when I need help with something, even harder when it's—well, it's not someone I've known for a long time." He looked up at him. "Anyway, thanks for the assist."

"Not a problem."

"I can smell the sour cream," Artur stated as he entered the kitchen, grinning. "I am very excited."

"Stop with the s-word," Abe said. "That word is verboten, *nein nicht*, nope in this house."

Jacob looked back and forth between the two of them and grinned. "Is this an applesauce-free zone?"

"I don't ever sneeze at anything parve," Abe replied with a laugh. "I *never* deny the power of applesauce."

"A knife to my heart," Artur said, with a shake of his head. "Applesauce is awful, and I will spend my life attempting to preach the power of sour cream."

"You mean the power of dairy," Jacob said. "I like parve. I think parve is so much more fascinating, but I can be persuaded otherwise in the right moment by the right chef."

And as they settled in, Artur taking coats to the closet, Jacob continued to talk. "What's this all about?" He gestured widely between himself and Artur.

"This guy has no poker face," Artur explained before Abe could get a word in edgewise. "And also I wanted to play poker."

"Things went horribly downhill on Saturday night," Abe clarified as he turned back to the stove, piling the pierogis, blintzes, and knishes onto a plate. "Three ice creams in and there was a misguided, horrible idea of a kiss."

Jacob shook his head, and shoved his hands into his pockets as if he was about to step in front of a board room. "I don't get it."

"It was a horrible idea," Abe said as he ran a towel across his forehead, "because apparently I have no poker face, and looked as if she'd hung the stars."

"Which is weird, why? Because you've never before explained to her how you felt?"

"They have a perennial failure to communicate," Artur interjected.

Jacob snorted. "I get it. Communication isn't the easiest thing in the world to handle when neither of you know what you want from the other person."

Artur folded his arms. "Explain."

"So from what I know of the situation, and fill me in if I'm wrong," Jacob's steel-blue eyes met Abe's. "She's trying to not want anything from you. And you're trying to figure out where she fits in your life."

Abe sighed. Deeply. "Yeah. That's what I'm afraid of."

"Now from my perspective, that's a surmountable obstacle," Jacob said.

What exactly was surmountable about that? "How?"

As they brought the food to the table, poured the drinks, Jacob began to explain. "You need to decide here and now that Batya's opinion about where you two stand is the most important, and that no matter what she decides, you're okay with it."

"But—"

Jacob shook his head. And there was a vehemence to his response. "No buts. No matter what. That choice has the potential to shatter you, and I know it might, but you need to be firm. Friends, more, less, whatever, Batya's decision is the most important one."

Which was an important perspective to think about.

Batya was the one who deserved the upper hand; because he was the one who was fixing the mistake, he was asking for forgiveness. He wanted to build something new. "It's only been a few days now that I've been living with the impact of the fact that I want...that I have feelings for her I'm willing to act on," he finally said. "She's been living with the result of my inability to tell her how I feel for a lot longer."

"Years," Artur added as he swiped a piece of a blintz through the sour cream. "Actual, literal years. Many of them."

"Wait," Jacob interjected. "You mean...?" He shook his head. "That's just...no."

"Let me get you up to speed," Artur interjected before Abe had a chance. "She had a crush, she told him how she felt, he completely blew the reply and sent her out of town for the last few years. And by few, I mean many."

Jacob once again turned to Abe. "You've been respecting boundaries since then, hence the tea."

Once again Abe nodded. "And the dry cleaning."

The realization ran across Jacob's face. "Which is why she didn't trust the dry cleaning. And instead you sent her..."

"Ice cream. After the classes. You know. To show her I was paying attention and to let her know the impact of her words, of the class, on me."

"And then what happened?"

As he told the story of Saturday's events, Artur tried not

to laugh as Jacob shook his head.

"Ooof. Okay. So," Jacob took a drink of his water. "You're going to need a lot more than a poker face to fix this. But a poker face is probably a good place to start."

Abe nodded. "I figured that. So we play cards, you both teach me poker face, or at least enough of one so I can go to class tomorrow and not scare the hell out of her."

Artur nodded. "That is a good choice. And then we all try to spin a dreidel on its top, because everybody tries every year."

And Abe was not even a little bit surprised when Jacob removed a dreidel from his pocket and spun it upside down.

Chapter Sixteen

BATYA DISCOVERED THAT thinking about what Anna had said on Sunday brought up a maelstrom of difficult emotions, not just passive resonance associated with a former crush, but also active emotions, the kind of feelings that reminded her how much what she'd felt about Abe had colored the way she'd seen so many of the events of her life.

At least the events that took place in Rivertown.

Unfortunately, understanding the problem didn't necessarily help fix it. Seeing him? Trying to figure out what she'd actually have to manage to say to him without reverting to being a teenager?

Terrifying.

And kissing him on Saturday had left her lips on fire.

This class was going to be impossible.

But there was a knock on the door, and as she went to answer it, once again, she saw the familiar uniform of the Rivertown Ice delivery people.

Once again, there was a cooler, a package, and a card. As usual, she opened the card first.

Batya,

I'm sending this one early because I have a feeling you're going to worry. And I realize that you have reason to be concerned, but let me assure you of the things I have control over.

1. *I crossed a few lines on Saturday and I'm sorry. I made you uncomfortable and that's the last thing I want to make you.*
2. *Your meat class later today will go swimmingly, even if I have to deliver a lecture myself. Which I won't, because Moshe's coming.*
3. *The ice cream is a bit unconventional, but I like it. I figured that the traditional symbol for teachers tied with the hope for a sweet new year would be appropriate no matter what.*

Abe

And when she opened the Apples and Honey flavor, she smiled. Maybe they were heading toward new beginnings. That, or she'd manage to make her way through class.

AFTER AN EXTENDED conversation with Moshe, they'd arranged to meet at the parking lot located just behind the high school before the class. Abe had expected some kind of chaos in the form of lingering high schoolers when he arrived, but when he drove up the hill and pulled into a spot, just a bit before their meeting time, there was nobody. Not even a trace of the straggler high schoolers, hanging around after practice, or the faint hint of music or smoke in the late November air.

This was going to be a mess.

Moshe was going to flake, the traffic would keep Jacob from fulfilling his promise, and Batya was going to lose this chance.

No.

This wasn't going to be a total disaster. All he wanted were things that would somehow manage to be slightly coherent. For Batya.

"Aaaabe!"

He turned to see Moshe standing behind him, his eyes bright and his smile big. "Oh thank God," he said.

"*Baruch hashem* for sure," Moshe replied, "but I wouldn't consider myself anything. So."

"Nu? What did you think?"

"I have to tell you," Moshe replied, that smile still broad, "that I watched the episodes. Lectures. And I liked what I saw. Good history of food, good stories, and good reactions from the class."

"I'm glad you did. She got a good bunch of speakers."

"Is this what you take me for?"

Abe smiled. And that was the crux of this, right? "You're someone who knows what he's doing, someone who understands the trade and what kosher meat is. You can give a talk any day."

Moshe nodded, reached up to wipe across his brow. "Excellent. So. Am I presenting alone?"

Abe shrugged. "I don't know. You may have to start presenting by yourself, but I don't know how long that's going to have to be."

"Nu?"

"A friend said he's got someone for you to present with, but they're battling traffic."

Moshe raised an eyebrow. "Traffic from where? Upstate? Cross the bridge?"

Abe shook his head. "Somewhere on Long Island, I think is what he said. I have no idea."

Moshe nodded. "Well," he said with a smile. "Let's talk a bit and then I'll start to get ready."

And that, Abe decided, was the best idea of all. Hopefully Batya would think so too.

BATYA FOUND HERSELF standing in the high school parking lot forty-five minutes before class was supposed to begin, slightly chilled and lost for words. Two cars in the parking lot, one car she recognized and one she didn't.

The one she recognized was Abe's.

She pulled into a space near his, trying desperately not to

have flashbacks to moments where she'd parked here before play practice or even quiz bowl rehearsal.

As she got out of the car, she looked around the parking lot, near the bright lights that illuminated the area.

Abe was sitting by himself on the curb.

He was looking somewhere, elsewhere, not at her it seemed. What was going on? Who else had met him?

But standing there staring, letting her mind go to places it shouldn't, wasn't the best of ideas. Instead, she walked toward him. "Hey," she said. "What's going on?"

"Waiting for Moshe."

She nodded. "What were you guys up to?"

Abe shrugged. "We wanted to go over a few things before you got here," he said as he stood. "He wanted to chat about what he was doing, what the expectations were, and what the class was like from someone who's been there."

"Makes sense," she said. "Thank you."

"You're welcome." He paused. "You know, you're going to do great tonight."

She couldn't help the way the corners of her mouth seemed to jump for joy, the smile clearly wanting to make itself known. "Thanks. I appreciate that." And then came the hard part. "I wanted to talk to you."

"Did you get the ice cream?"

"I loved it," she said. "It was great. Thank you."

"You're welcome."

She wanted to stand here, comfortable with him, but she

didn't. "I wanted to apologize," she said, yanking the words out of herself as if she'd been playing with silly putty. "Because you have the wrong impression. You didn't make me uncomfortable. I did. And I want to make it up to you."

"You know you don't have to make it up to me," he said. "Your feelings are your feelings, and if for a second you felt I didn't respect them, you'd have every right to leave and not come back."

She raised an eyebrow. But this wasn't the conversation she wanted to have. "Saturday was great, but it was confusing. How much time do we have? Where's Moshe?"

"Bathroom," he replied. "So we might have time."

She raised an eyebrow. "Might?"

He nodded, and as she was going to say something, the sound of tires on the concrete busted through the conversation, and bright lights heralded a familiar car.

Jacob.

And suddenly, all of the conversations she wanted to have with Abe got shoved to the side in favor of the conversation that they were about to have.

And that was going to be interesting. Because if Jacob had done what he'd promised, there was no telling how Abe was going to react.

ABE HALF WONDERED what Jacob would say if he'd told him

what his arrival had interrupted, but then there would be a possibility that he'd drive out just as quickly as he drove in.

"I think you should brace yourself," Batya said.

Which came out of nowhere. "I don't know who Jacob told you he was trying to convince," he said, as if he needed to demonstrate he wasn't completely out of his depth here, "but he told me he'd done it."

She *looked* at him, and it was obvious from her expression that she knew who Jacob asked. She was the instructor, after all. "So he didn't tell you? Didn't give you any ideas?"

Once again Abe shook his head. "He said it was going to be hard—that's all I know." The part where Jacob admitted he wasn't sure he was going to be able to manage it was something Abe kept to himself. "I'm prepared to be surprised at whatever he pulls out of his hat."

The car door opened.

The man's timing was impeccable, Abe had to admit.

"I'm no magician," Jacob said with a smile. "Just good when my friends are in a pinch."

Abe checked his watch—Jacob had managed to get to the high school before the estimate. "You beat traffic. How did you manage to get here so fast?"

Jacob shrugged. "I told my friend here that we needed to leave earlier than he'd intended, so we did and here we are."

"Here we are," said another voice.

A familiar voice. A voice he hadn't heard in four years.

"Mr. Goldberg?"

"Avram Newman," Mr. Goldberg said with a smile, as if absolutely no time had passed since Shabbat lunches spent at the deli counter when his feet didn't reach the ground, since two snot-nosed kids stopped off at the deli for snacks with their homework between regular school and Hebrew school at Rivertown Synagogue on Wednesdays.

"Pastrami club, pickles and mustard. How are you?"

"I'm good, sir," he said, struggling to hold himself together in the face of someone who remembered his order, even if the deli he'd ordered it from had closed four years before. "I'm good."

"It's good to see you. And you, Miss Averman. The weekly ask for the order nobody could figure out, but turned out to be mashed potato fried with onions and eggs."

Batya smiled sheepishly, the blush coloring her cheeks in ways that made his heart warm. "I wanted my bikeleh."

"Which was tradition, of course."

He didn't know her deli traditions, but knowing she had an order made Abe feel closer to her, as if she'd bonded with the place in the same way he had.

"It was," she said. "It was. I'm sorry I made you work so hard to find it."

Mr. Goldberg smiled. "It was, of course, not as bad as the character who came in after Hebrew school to slurp his sour cream as well as his borscht."

And in a second, Abe turned to meet Batya's eyes. "Artur," they both said with a smile.

"Ach, Mr. Rabinovich. Will I be seeing him tonight?"

Abe shook his head. "No. He'd send his regards if he knew you were here."

Of course, that exchange did not in any way prepare him for what happened when Moshe arrived. "Tateh Goldberg?"

"Moshele? Is that you? Little Moshele?"

And as the two embraced, what seemed like surrogate father to son, Abe gestured toward Jacob to join the group.

Slowly, carefully, and reluctantly, Jacob came over to join them, crossing the parking lot.

"Dude," Abe said with a smile. "I don't know how you did this, but thank you."

Jacob nodded. "Not a problem. You're a friend," he said.

And then Abe watched Jacob look between them, and clearly come to some decision. "I think I'm probably going to head out, take care of some stuff, you know. Be back in about an hour to pick Aaron up, drive him back."

And just as Abe was going to say something, he saw Batya vehemently shake her head. "No. Absolutely not. You're here, so come into class."

"Watch those guys work their magic," Abe said, pointing to Moshe and Mr. Goldberg as they huddled in the corner, talking presumably about anything from memories to strategy. "Warm the desk next to mine. Though," Abe turned toward Batya, "speaking of desk warming, do you know if Linda or someone from the committee is going to watch tonight?"

"I don't know."

Abe nodded, glad to do something for her. "Then I'll take a run in. See if anybody's there. And when I come back, I can warn you, we can prep for this and then…"

"You would?" she asked.

Abe nodded. "Yes. I would."

And as he headed off, he made sure to salute her.

BATYA SIGHED AND shook her head as Abe headed into the school. She needed to take control.

This was *her* class. Not Abe's or Jacob's or anybody else's. There were instructors in the corner she had to speak to.

"You going to be okay?"

"Yep. I'm going to be," she said firmly; fake it until you make it had to be her guiding principle at this point. "Thank you, by the way."

Jacob shook his head. "It's not a problem. I made the offer; I was prepared to follow through."

"I appreciate the fact you did. Both of those things."

But even though Abe had talked to Moshe, she had no idea what Jacob had said to Mr. Goldberg. "What did you tell him, by the way?"

"What do you mean?"

"When Abe gets back," she said, "I'm going to have to

brief Moshe and Mr. Goldberg for the class, tell them more specifically what I expect from them. But if you did some of my basic legwork for me, like Abe seems to have done with Moshe, I'll need less prep time."

"I told Mr. Goldberg to watch that second lecture, see how the class worked. Is that okay?"

Batya nodded, relieved. "Perfect, thank you."

"Not a problem," he said. "Are you good? Do you want me to head over to the Caf and Nosh and get you tea or something?"

Even her favorite mint tea from the Caf and Nosh wasn't going to help her get through tonight's class. She'd have to do it through strength of will, especially now.

If the class and the fry-off went well, she'd be the host of a television show, forced to determine on camera what was really going on with people, and ask them the kinds of questions that would allow them to open up and tell the stories of their family food history. And if she couldn't manage to defuse the hovering mass that was her friend's fiancé, she'd have no chance.

"It's fine," she said. "Really. Better than the ridiculous nonsense they're pulling with the Shadow Squad, sword or no sword."

He smiled, his shoulders dropping. Their shared Shadow Squad fandom never ceased to amaze her, not to mention the fact that the man actually had bought a replica of Mr. Shadow's sword at a Comic Con the year before.

"Speaking of time and space," he eventually said, "Anna's got a thing with her M school group in the city tonight, but she wanted me to tell you that if you want her here—"

Once again, Batya shook her head. Firmly.

Vehemently.

The very last thing she needed was for him to involve her best friend in this.

"No," she said, maybe a bit more firmly than she'd expected, but it was important. "It's fine. She doesn't need to leave a gathering you know is some kind of bridal shower."

"It's technically a mentorship meeting," he said with a smile. "They've got a few aspiring history majors and potential curators they're helping with college applications, internships, and a few other things."

Which was, in fact, what Anna had told her earlier that day, but at the same time, the timing was strange. She raised an eyebrow.

"But yes," he said with a laugh, "you're right. I absolutely suspect it's also some kind of bridal shower."

"Either way," she said, "tonight is going to go well. You can tell her about how well I did afterward."

"Fair enough," he said as Abe joined them.

"Coast is clear?" she asked.

"Transparent," Abe replied with a smile she felt all the way down to her toes. "Extremely transparent."

"Excellent," she said. "You guys stay here and hang out for a while. I'm going to go and prep the lecturers."

And full of excitement, she headed toward Moshe and Mr. Goldberg.

She was going to kick some serious tuchus tonight. She couldn't wait to get started.

Chapter Seventeen

A BE WAS STILL flummoxed.

In the face of her triumph Wednesday night, Batya invited him over on Sunday afternoon.

Flummoxed, excited, everything. Full of emotions that made every single bit of sense and no sense at the very same time.

As he was heading up the steps to her house, Abe could, in fact, admit that he was nervous.

But Batya's smile as she opened the door was welcoming, her eyes bright in a way that he hadn't expected or counted on. It felt...right.

"Glad you could make it," she said.

As if he'd even make any other plans knowing that she wanted him over. "Glad to be here," he said as he followed her into the house.

He'd never been inside her home. And strangely enough, it reminded him of his own house, the one he'd spent his childhood in and now was back to spend at least this part of his adulthood in.

"Do you want to sit down? Do you...?"

He turned toward her, seeing the frenetic movements in her hands, the random brightness in her eyes. Was she nervous too?

"It's me," he said as calmly as he could. "You really don't have to pretend I'm some kind of important guest."

"But you are," she said. "You're going to judge my latkes."

He couldn't hold back the laugh. "You're kidding me."

Batya shook her head. "No," she said. "I'm not."

He grinned. "Okay. So you're making me latkes?"

She nodded. "I am, only—"

He raised an eyebrow. "What?"

"I don't feel inspired," she said. "I wasn't trying to be this unprepared, but apparently I am."

"What seems to be the trouble?"

She walked to the front window of the house, leaving him to stand there, following Jacob's advice. He waited, wondering what was wrong. "I don't feel like it's Hanukkah even though it's close."

"I see." He looked around the room, the kitchen, the windowsill.

Nothing.

He wasn't surprised. But all the same, he smiled.

"What? What's missing?"

He laughed. "I think I understand why you're having trouble getting into the Hanukkah spirit."

"That is not a sentence I ever thought I'd hear you say."

He shrugged. "Sorry, but it's true. You're not inspired to make latkes, even though, as they say, 'tis the season. Ergo, you're not in the Hanukkah spirit."

"I'll take it." She laughed. "Now explain why I'm not feeling the proverbial spirit of the season."

"Well," he said. "Take a look around. What don't you see?"

He waited as she took a breath, then turned around, staring at the room, at the kitchen, at the empty space where he'd expect a menorah.

"Holy crap."

"Do you see it?"

She nodded. "I'm such a draikopf, you know? Like my grandmother said."

"Your grandmother or your aunt?"

"My Tante, actually."

"What's the deal?"

She laughed, and he liked who she was when she could breathe. He always had. "We don't have any decorations. My parents keep all of their stuff in Florida and my tante has her own."

Abe tapped his chin with his index finger. "Interesting. Do you even have a menorah of your own?"

"In a storage bin somewhere, I think. Nothing readily accessible," she admitted.

"Well then," Abe replied. "Let's go."

"Let's go where?"

"Bullseye. There's a big one not far from here. I'll drive."

She followed him to the car, and she didn't argue. He didn't want to fight with her either.

He opened the car door; she got in. It was comfortable, having her in his car, in his space again.

"You're not going to make me listen to Hanukkah music on the way to Bullseye, are you?"

"I wasn't going to," he admitted. "But you know, I might as well."

She rolled her eyes, and he couldn't help but laugh. "Fighting traffic fueled by ma'oz tzur?"

"Moving from lane to lane, spinning like a s'vivon?"

"Serenaded over lunch by latke songs everywhere?"

In the end, he didn't play the Hanukkah music he'd stashed in his glove compartment, but he did flip the radio dial.

"Modern Day Maccabees," she said with a laugh. "I kinda love hearing this."

"I celebrate. I celebrate Ha_Nu_Kah," he sang, grooving along with the David Streit classic as she hit the dashboard, grinning. "It's been however many years and I still get a kick out of this song."

"Menorahs glowing, on a windowsill," she sang along with Zack Weisler on the next song, "snow boots lined up at the door."

"Hanukkah songs, being sung by a choir, and kids playing dreidel games."

"I love this," Batya gushed, her eyes bright, her cheeks slightly red. "I think that's my favorite thing, you know?"

Singing with him? Spending time with him? Being close enough to touch?

"Listening to the radio, hearing that song, knowing it's ours."

The global, representational aspect, of course. Not the personal, emotional aspect. Never that.

But maybe at some point it would be?

He snuffed that candle out, focusing instead on the here and now before she started to wonder if he'd checked out, and changed the subject. "I do know. Like how it feels entering this fry-off."

"I don't know what I'm doing. I don't know if I'm good enough to host."

Abe pulled into the parking lot, found a space beyond the store, and stared at the red-brick buildings before he turned back toward her. "You're kidding."

Batya shook her head. "I'm not. George Gold has shows on Meal Network. They wanted ratings from him, and anything he touches on Meal Network gets watched. Me? I'm just a girl with a blog. I'm nothing special."

"Everybody starts somewhere," Abe said. "George Gold started somewhere."

"But I feel like I'm letting everybody down. The town needs a boost now, not a wannabe."

"You're totally not a wannabe," he said, grinning.

"They're going to give you a legitimate shot, and you deserve every bit of this. I'll prove it to you."

She looked at him dubiously, but he already knew what he was doing. He had a plan.

And he couldn't wait to execute it.

BATYA HAD NO idea what had happened or what Abe expected of her. Was he trying to turn her into everybody's favorite Hanukkah fairy?

Because that wasn't her personality; it never had been. She was proud of being Jewish, loved celebrating the holidays, all of them, with her friends and family. But celebrating any particular holiday had never defined her identity, at least not in the tentpole sort of way that Hanukkah had defined other people's.

And for some reason, that made her nervous.

What was Abe doing?

Was he playing the role of the huge Hanukkah fan, teaching the person who'd dismissed the holiday for any number of reasons the real, true spirit of Hanukkah?

Not that Hanukkah spirit was actually a thing. Batya had always thought that Hanukkah was where you found it, that the holiday didn't have much in the way of defined expectations for a reason. Whether you celebrated it in a big way or a small one, with family or with an entire town, as long as you remembered to celebrate it, it was okay with her.

And as she crossed the shopping center parking lot in the early December cold, she found herself once again questioning Abe's motives. "I'm not Sarah," she said in warning as they stepped into the store. It was big, filled with the first snippets of decorations from a bunch of different holidays that took place during the month.

"What?" Confusion was written across Abe's face. "You think this is a problem for me?"

"For Sarah," she said, "Hanukkah is life. It's everything, but I'm not like that."

"Well, that's good," Abe said, "because this isn't about the whole Hanukkah lifestyle. This is 358 other days of the year sorta style, minus those eight particular nights."

She snorted. Only Abe.

Only Abe was still a dangerous thought. She needed to remember that. "Okay. So the eight are what we need to focus on, right?"

Abe shook his head. "Not necessarily." They stopped in front of the cookbooks. "You know she started as a catering chef," he said as he took out Katie Feldman's latest "One of the many cooking caterers who was in a kitchen for big events. One of the guests sent in a last-minute dietary—"

"Yes," Batya said. She was not going to be mansplained, even if the intentions were good. "One of the guests sent in a last-minute dietary allergy or whatever, and she was the only one on the staff who knew how to fix it. It kept happening, and she got famous for fixing people's mistakes. Which is lovely but entirely unrelated to the subject at hand."

"My point," Abe said, smiling, "is that she started somewhere. I think she's also judging the fry-off."

And there were her nerves again. "You should have quit while you were ahead with that one."

He laughed. "I'm sorry. I'll try not to remind you about judges for the fry-off."

"It's not that I'm not excited about the fact they're judging," she said, once again giving in to the impulse to explain. "Far from that. It's that I don't want to be reminded of who I'll be in front of when I completely mess up."

Abe shook his head, and there was a kindness in his eyes. "You're not going to mess up. And," he paused, reached for something on the shelf, "you may not need this, but I do."

The shirt he pulled from the shelf and placed in front of her read Varsity Matzah Ball Squad.

"Oh my God," she managed, the words tumbling out of her mouth faster than she could grab the shirt. "We need these." Then she realized the import of what she'd said. "You know. For the quiz bowl crew."

"Crew's not here," he said with a smile. "You know."

She raised an eyebrow. "You want an inside joke?"

"Yes," he said. "I want we should have an inside joke. Just ours."

She put the shirt down and stared at him. "Why?"

He looked down and away from her before he spoke.

"For the last however many years, the thing that's tied us together is—was—a wound. I know you're not ready—"

"I will never be ready to discuss it," she said, making her feelings as clear and as definitive as she could in those eight words.

"Fair enough, and yes. That's what I meant." And when he looked up at her, his eyes were emerald bright. Beautiful in ways she hadn't let herself think about. "So maybe an inside joke, aside from ice cream class summaries and some spilled tea, might be the beginnings of new ties?"

"Putting Band-Aids covered in glitter or cartoon characters on wounds don't heal anything."

"Not by themselves," he said. "But maybe, just maybe, they cover the wound, which we've kept poking at for more than ten years. Maybe it needs some space to heal."

She blew out a breath as she tried to get her feelings together, to give herself reason not to yell at him in the middle of a Bullseye store. "Why? What's the point of healing a wound like that?"

She followed his fingers toward the bigger display of Hanukkah stuff, the shirts forgotten. "The biggest point," he said, "is that every single interaction between us is affected by that. I can't go back and change what happened, and I don't want to hurt you again by making you talk about it when you're not ready to."

"But?"

"But maybe we can start to try to figure out who we are,

who we want to be now. Not just for us, not just between us, but for everybody else we're friends with."

"Because everybody's going to be talking about us, about this for the rest of our lives," she said, remembering Anna's advice. "Because you're making friends with the fiancé of one of my best friends."

"Which," he said as he pulled down a pack of plastic dreidels, "is the weirdest thing. For a few different reasons. But it's working out."

It was working out for many reasons, one of which was that it let her see him with people who weren't from Rivertown. Someone like Jacob couldn't be the convenient lens of perception she'd known for most of her life. And because Abe was spending time with different people, he acted differently.

Which was not a bad thing. The fact that seeing him around her Hollowville friends didn't make her twitchy was, in fact, a very good thing.

Which led her to words she didn't think she'd actually said to him.

"I never really thanked you, by the way."

"Me? For what?"

"For Moshe. For saving my butt."

He laughed as he reached for a box of beeswax candles, making her smile as Zack Weisler sang of the joys of lighting candles and spinning dreidels on their tops. "I thought this was your way of thanking me."

"We do need to figure this whole thing out. For us. Not for anybody else, or our friendships or theirs, but for *us*."

"Any particular reason that inspired you?"

She saw a box of latke mix out of the corner of her eye. But instead of taking it off the shelf, she grabbed a menorah she'd been eyeing. "All's fair in love and latkes, of course."

The sound of his laugh was enough to warm her for the rest of her life. And maybe then some.

ABE WASN'T TOO upset with Batya for not letting him hang the ridiculous decorations he'd convinced her to buy. But all the same, as she put up the menorah, he turned to the stereo system and put on a Hanukkah playlist, full of fun parody songs and some really cool renditions of a few traditional songs.

"You're going to do fine," he said as he came back to the kitchen.

Her smile was genuine. He knew her smiles, of course. This one set him on fire.

"How do you do it?"

He choked on whatever remnants of his lunch still sat in his throat. "What do you mean?"

Full blown smile, bright eyes, she was dangerous and un-leashed in a way she'd never been around him before. And he liked it.

"How do you make latkes? What did you think?"

Now it was his turn to laugh. "I don't know. Figured it would be something hotter than the space above the menorah on the eighth night."

"I can't take you anywhere," she said, continuing to chop something.

He stepped closer and gawked. "You're cutting potatoes by hand?"

"Maybe I'm a traditionalist."

He shook his head. "No. A masochist is what you are."

She snorted. "Maybe I don't have a food processor."

"I can go get mine if you want."

"Why don't you help me chop?"

He considered the idea, and then took a knife, joining her as she chopped potatoes to the sound of a parody song's joyful recitation of a recipe for latkes.

"We're cutting onions here too?"

"I am," she said, "but only one."

He nodded. "Do you cry over onions?"

"Why? Would the fact that I cry over chopped vegetables be a problem?"

He smiled and took the onion himself, removing the peel and dicing it as carefully and as quickly as he could. "There. We have an onion."

She nodded. "Thank you. Next?"

He laughed. "I think I should be offended. Do you even know what to do?"

She raised an eyebrow. "I know how to make latkes," she said. "I was just…"

He nodded. "Testing me. Sure. That's fine."

"Making you cut the onion." He couldn't keep his eyes off her, watching as she stirred the mixture, the chopped potatoes and the onions he'd diced. "Pass me the breadcrumbs."

"Why breadcrumbs?"

"I like them the best," she said. "I've tried matzo meal, I've tried panko and flour, but nothing sops up that water like these guys."

"Makes sense. Now what?"

"The egg."

"No chicken?"

"Not in this house. I'm giving you sour cream space."

"Very slick. But unnecessary considering I only like sour cream on blintzes. Kosher?"

She shrugged. "My parents are, so I'm doing this for them. Their house, their kitchen. I don't like breaking someone else's rules even if they're not here."

"And what is your choice?"

Once again, as if she was on the edge of a precipice, she shrugged. "I don't know. I haven't decided what it means to me. If I'm making traditional food choices like cholent and chicken soup or Shabbas dinner and kugel and all of the foods we grew up with, then yes. But not when I'm eating food that wasn't created under our guidelines."

She paused as if she was waiting for him to say something. He didn't. He wasn't going to.

"Is that weird?"

Abe shrugged. "I have been keeping kosher, mostly because I need to be in order for the barbecue. I need to separate my meat and my milk in my house exclusively as long as I'm cooking. It doesn't feel right if I don't, much less anything outside the house. It makes things harder, and there are things I miss with a fierceness, but it works for me."

"No bacon?"

"Turkey bacon, lamb bacon, beef bacon, soy bacon, all of those things."

"No cheeseburgers?"

"No chicken parmigiana either, which, by the way, is a thing I miss."

"No vegan cheese?"

He shook his head. "Unfortunately." And then he peeked into the bowl, cutting off the conversation before he convinced himself to do something ridiculous. "That looks about right," he said. "So what do you want me to do?"

"Oil," she said pointing to a pan on the stove. "That's the pan."

He picked up the bottle of olive oil, poured some in the bottom of the pan. "Why olive?"

"Again, family thing, but also I like it better."

"Fair enough. Who am I to argue?"

She laughed, a tinkling sound that made him smile. "I

don't know why you're being nice."

"Why is it suspicious that I'm nice?"

"You're not fighting with me."

He wondered where the surprise in her voice came from, and instead of fighting her, raised an eyebrow. "What would be the point of fighting with you in your own kitchen after we decided to build bridges?"

"I don't know."

"Exactly," he said. "It doesn't exist."

"It doesn't exist."

And that was the worst time to remember he had oil in a pan on a stove.

THERE WAS A bubbly soda feeling inside of Batya. It was fun to be able to feel it as opposed to spending all of her energy fighting it, suppressing it, and making it burn her from the inside.

She wasn't analyzing him; she'd spent too much of her life doing that. He was having a good time? That was great.

But more importantly, she was.

He was staring at the oil, so she changed the music to some jumpy, bumpy excited dance music, and grooved her way back to the table. Napkins, applesauce, sour cream, tea in glasses, and some of the ice cream he'd sent her was waiting for dessert.

"I think it's ready," he said. And so she meandered her way over, stopping near the bowl, taking out her scoop.

"You're making latkes with an ice cream scoop?"

She laughed. "I'm measuring the mixture with an ice cream scoop. People use it with cookie dough, why not this?"

"Because it's weird."

The sound of his laugh made her smile in a way that she hadn't been able to let herself in a long time. Or at least, she hadn't let herself feel things around Abe the same way she did around everybody else because she'd been so scared by how much she felt about him, how much she cared for him. Not until now.

And as she scooped the last latke into the pan, she found herself thinking of—

"Be careful."

"Sorry," she said. "Thinking about a bunch of things."

He nodded. "Hopefully some of them are the latkes."

"Yeah. They are."

"Traditional latkes. I'm sorry I didn't bring my applesauce."

"Your applesauce?"

He nodded. "I made some, decided I wanted to see if I could."

"Bring it—or bring me some the next time we're in a place we can admit we saw each other."

"Are we going to be secret friends?"

"Maybe we need to test these new bridges of ours and

hang out around a smaller group of people who know us as we are now, or at least people who are pretty good at seeing past the past? Like maybe Artur and my Hollowville friends?"

He nodded, and she wondered why that felt like they'd just cleared a huge obstacle. "I like that. We can just be— before the fry-off, before people start to tie us together in ways they shouldn't."

She liked his line of thought. Even more, she liked the fact they seemed to be on the same page. "We can figure out what we are to each other, what we want to be. By ourselves."

As he brought the latkes to the table, she smiled at him. "Thank you."

"What are you thanking me for?"

"Understanding what I meant, coming over, and…just being. Spending time with me."

The small smile he gave her in return was adorable. "I figure," he said, "we've been in a pressure cooker for years. It will be nice to know each other as adults without the pressure of peeping peeps."

She laughed. "Peeping peeps is a phrase."

"Good one?"

She nodded. "Yeah." And then he stepped toward her, letting her move in to the circle of his arms. "Can I kiss you?"

"Absolutely," he said.

And so she carefully pressed her lips to his, the taste of his breath bringing her home, the feel of his fingers as they navigated her jawline, the way he knew how to get around the earpieces of her glasses, the sensation of...

The sound of her stomach growling.

"Well," she said as she broke the kiss, "I guess it's time."

"It is. And this time it's not going to make us nervous."

Nervous was the least of what it was making her. And she was completely okay with any and all the emotions he was making her feel.

Chapter Eighteen

B ATYA HAD NOT been able to focus on anything since she
got the email from George Gold, not her breakfast, or
her laundry, or the piece she was supposed to write for the
website.

The. George. Gold.

He didn't just email her, of course. He'd emailed every
participant in the fry-off, including her. However, the
separate email he'd sent her was going to derail her day, if
not her life.

Same address as the other, same subject line, but the text!
The text stood out; his words would be burned in her brain
for the rest of her life. Words like:

**Call me if you need anything. Your website is killer,
and I'm here to help if you have any questions about
working with the crew for this. And when it's over,
I'd like to talk to you about some other things.**

I'd like to talk to you about other things.
Holy crap.
Also, working with the crew?
Did he actually tell her she was going to be hosting?

Thankfully, Sarah was lecturing that night, so when Batya asked her friend to come a bit earlier, Sarah agreed.

"How are you doing?"

Batya sighed, gone from thinking about the impact George Gold would have on her life, to a conversation about the panic attack she'd had, and probably the fact that she'd had to take Jacob up on a favor he'd offered in order to save the fourth class. Then again, there was friendship. Asking for the details, filling the holes, making sure things were better than the storyteller, probably Anna in this case, had made it seem. "You heard?"

"Of course I did. I was worried—hassled but worried."

"I'm better," Batya said. If she'd actually compared how she'd felt two weeks before and now, there would be a world of difference, but all of it good. "It was hard, not gonna lie. But Abe was there."

"Abe? The guy with the tea the first day? The zombie crush?"

Batya nodded. "Yeah. Him. He's been nice. It's been a comfort."

"Is he here?"

"Any particular reason?"

"Isaac wanted to know."

Batya shook her head. Small group of friends, small group of problems. "Not yet, but he will be. Dinner afterward?"

Sarah didn't answer right away. But Batya wasn't offended; this wasn't just her friend but the newly appointed chair of a festival that was going into final-stage preparations. "Unless someone calls me after class with a problem, then yes. We should, though, especially considering it's going to be all latkes all the time for you and all festival for me starting in the next few days."

As she was about to answer, Batya heard a familiar voice. "Hey."

She turned toward Abe, couldn't help the smile. "Hi there. Dinner?"

"Shouldn't stay late, but that works."

She'd spent her life hiding the smile that naturally showed up around him. Now she didn't have to, and it felt comfortable. Being open about how she felt around him, and him not making her feel like crossing the country.

That was a joy, one she'd never take for granted.

"Good." Sarah smiled. "Glad to hear it."

"Oh," she managed. "Right. Abe, this is Sarah Goldman, one of my closest friends from Hollowville. Sarah, this is Abe Newman, one of the competitors and someone I've known most of my life."

"That language sounds suspiciously like words Anna used when introducing me to Jacob for the third time in my memory."

Batya laughed. "Wellll," she said.

Sarah seemed to get the gist, and if she didn't, at least she wasn't going to push it. "Anyway, you can go and find my assistant, who's sitting somewhere and going to be bored. Keep him company till it's time for him to help."

Abe nodded, and before he left he focused on Batya. "Later?" he said to her.

"Later."

And as he turned to leave, she smiled, trying not to completely loose her mind and kiss him in front of everybody. "So yeah," she told her friend. "That's him."

"I can see," Sarah said with a laugh. "This is going to be interesting."

And thankfully when Sarah said it, it sounded like the good kind of interesting, not the sort of interesting that came with the promise of disaster.

>>>><<<<

ABE HEADED UP the aisle, stopping in front of his usual seat, smiling at a few of the other attendees, soon to be his competition.

Which was both exciting and concerning at the same time.

The fry-off was on Saturday.

Only days to Hanukkah.

"You figured it out."

Abe was startled at first, but he turned to his left, only to see the seat on the aisle filled by a guy with big shoulders. "I'm sorry?"

"The dry cleaning."

Ah, this man had been part of the group he'd met on the eve of Batya's audition, one of the Hollowville group. "Riiight," he managed. "I did, I think."

"Sarah is speaking to you, so you figured it out," the man said. "Which means I'm hoping you play Pictionary as well as poker."

Abe raised an eyebrow. "Pictionary?"

"Name's Isaac Lieberman," he said—clearly, he knew Abe hadn't remembered his name. "My game is Pictionary, but my friends and I play on the nondominant hand."

"I don't get it."

"You have to see it to believe it," Isaac said with a laugh as he settled in. "Seeing artists try to play Pictionary with their nondominant hand is a trip. You'll come and play with my friends at one point." He paused. "You live in the city?"

And then Abe understood. This guy was reaching out in some way. Which was nice but strange. "I did. Had a one-bedroom, liked it. But I needed more space when I decided I wanted to make more barbecue, so I sold it a few years ago. I live back in Rivertown now, not far from here actually."

Isaac nodded. "Interesting. But cool. You moved for your art, which I will definitely have to taste at some point. For Pictionary, we'll hang at Sarah's place—she's in Hollowville—and we'll have barbecue. But not till after Hanukkah."

"She's got to be really busy now."

"Yep. Unbelievably so. It's great for her, gives her something she loves, and I love it for her. Which is also why I'm here." He smiled. "I don't get out often."

Abe laughed. Now that was a sense of humor he could deal with. It also made him think about what Batya's life would be like after the competition, what his life would be like after the competition.

What *their* life would be like.

Not necessarily the best direction for his thoughts, not then, not yet. And so he forced himself back on task, back to the conversation. "Before I came up here, both Batya and Sarah said we should make plans for tonight, though. Dinner? Dessert?"

"Sounds good," Isaac said. "Where? Here? Hollowville? I know Sarah might get pulled into late committee stuff, but I'm totally ready for whatever you're up to. I'm not going back to the city till tomorrow."

So many ideas. "We'll see what Sarah and Batya want," he said. "I'm pretty open."

"Depends on how late this goes." Isaac smiled, "And that's my cue."

As Isaac headed to the aisle, Abe focused on Batya and the beginning of the last class.

"Thank you all so much for everything you've given me and this series. Tonight's lecture will also be available on the Hollowville Hanukkah Festival's website. We urge you to stop by the festival once it opens, to take advantage of some of the opportunities it offers."

And then, the class, who by this point knew what to expect, grew quiet again. "And now, it is my privilege to introduce tonight's lecturer. She is many things: friend, assistant manager at the Tales from Hollowville bookstore in Hollowville, as well as the newly minted chairperson of the Hollowville Hanukkah Festival committee. Please welcome Sarah Goldman."

Sarah came to the front of the stage. "Repeat after me, everybody," she said. "I celebrate Hanukkah!"

Abe laughed, as he and the rest of the class replied, "I celebrate Hanukkah."

"Because this is the last lecture and the culmination of everything, you're going to learn how all of the presentations apply to your favorite holiday and mine." And of course, the guest lecturer for the evening flipped a switch and her sweater lit up. "Hanukkah."

As Isaac headed to the front of the room, Abe found himself riveted, not only to the lecture Sarah was giving but also the way Batya was able to relax into the moment, lean in, and listen. There were no stress lines on Batya's face; she wasn't reaching up to wipe the back of her neck. She was still clearly nervous, opening and closing her hands as if they were fists, then shoving them in the pockets of her pants, but she was managing it.

Which was as much of a gift as Sarah's lecture; how she managed to talk about Hanukkah food in ways he had never thought about before. How the applesauce versus sour cream debate hinged on the difference between which food was considered to be parve and which was considered dairy, how soofganiyot dough differed from challah dough, how cultures around the world fried meat and dough to make their own unique celebrations.

"Because again, remember, what makes a Hanukkah food? I want to hear you!"

"It has to be fried," the class yelled happily.

He made a note to see if he could check out the Hanukkah festival's food court area.

"And one of the things I will suggest is that you do some research beyond this class, and take a look at the kind of Hanukkah foods eaten by Jewish communities all over the world, as well as the foods adapted or created by inventive, excited chefs. Oil and a frying pan are a cooking technique, not a limitation. And no two cultures celebrate Hanukkah with the same food."

And that was where he got the idea, carefully switching from his notes app to his phone to send Leo a quick text.

Thankfully, his friend agreed. This was going to be fun.

THE CLASS FELT good, which was something Batya hadn't expected to say after the disaster two weeks before, at least not about it in any other way than it was over.

But last week had been a turning point. And this week? This week was special.

Isaac joined them, carrying the props he'd been using during the lecture itself. "This was great," he said. "Really great."

"I'm glad you thought so," she replied. "Thanks for helping out tonight."

"No problem."

But the best part was when Abe came down to join them. "You were good," he said with a smile as he put his arm around her. This time, clearly understanding the message she was sending her friends, and fully comfortable with it, she put her head on his shoulder.

"Felt good," she said.

"So," Sarah interjected with a grin, "did someone promise me dinner?"

"Yes!" Batya turned toward Abe and Isaac. "Any ideas?"

"Yep." And then he gave her a look, a half-smug, half-familiar look.

There was only one place he ever seemed to talk about with a look like that on his face. Fratelli's. Leo's. "You're kidding, right?"

Abe shook his head. "We're going to Fratelli's," he said. "Italian. Good stuff."

Which should have been predictable. Leo's was basically Abe's second home, and from her Rivertown days, hers as well.

And if anybody could make sure they'd have a good night, it would be Leo. Even if he'd spend a lot of the night giving Abe, and her, the business.

But she was still unsure about spending time with Abe and the tentative hand he offered, even if the entire restaurant would be their safe zone. She took it as she headed out of the school, of course, but she was still nervous.

Even as she drove to the restaurant, she found herself trying to think through all of this.

Was it real?

Was it possible?

Yes, she decided as she pulled into a parking space at Fratelli's, got out of her car and went to go meet Abe, Sarah, and Isaac.

She and Abe were possible.

And as they walked into Fratelli's with Sarah and Isaac, it felt concrete, like the beginning of something beautiful.

IT WASN'T THAT far a drive from the high school to Fratelli's, and it was a route Abe could take in his sleep, but this particular version of the drive made him nervous enough to blast his favorite band from New Jersey, with their trademark riffs and strong chords.

Still, when he pulled into the parking lot, his heart started to pound, and he could feel the tension starting to collect

STACEY AGDERN

in his shoulders.

Why the heck was he so nervous?

Because this would be the first time Leo would actually see him and Batya now. Navigating this new stage of their lives.

Right. Feelings he felt comfortable expressing, hands touching, lips touching…

And it was *happening.*

He pulled into a space, and got out of the car, walking toward the small group that had assembled just under the awning.

"You're here," Batya said, grinning with anticipation.

He smiled back at her. "You'd think I'd miss this?"

She laughed as he put an arm around her.

"I'm excited," Sarah said. "I've never been here before."

"Food's great," he said by way of introduction. "We're getting some comfort food he doesn't usually serve everybody. So it's even better."

He saw the dubious expression on Isaac's face, but he decided not to answer.

"We went to school together," Batya added, picking up the thread he would have used. "Leo was on the quiz team too."

Isaac's eyebrow was still raised, and his expression was still dubious.

"He can be trusted," Abe said, as he opened the door, jingling the bells as they had for years. "Despite the fact that

I've been giving him the business about spice for years."

"And I have been keeping secrets from him longer," Leo said, his eyes twinkling as they entered the restaurant.

He recognized that expression too; mischief and interrogations about romantic relationships and secrets would come later *if* he survived. Death by pasta, apparently.

"Leo Fratelli," he said by way of introduction.

"Sarah Goldman," Sarah said. "I'm looking forward to tonight. Abe said comfort food?"

"Oh, did he?"

That look meant trouble. The kind of trouble when you realized your best friend had been planning the practical joke he was about to unleash for years.

"I did," Abe said, trying to get Leo back on track, or at the very least doing his best to figure out what the heck his friend was up to. "What's going on?"

"So," Leo said with a smile, "I could do my comfort food, and have you complain I'm showing off."

"You *are* a show-off," Abe said, the response coming off his tongue as easily as it had been for more than half his life. But this is how it worked with them. Always.

Never let your best friend forget the mess he made of a heralded triple-decker lasagna, even though he'd been twelve when he'd tried it.

"Or—" Leo grinned, deviating from the routine for the first time in his life.

What was going on?

"I could *actually* show off and maybe do something fun that I've been hiding."

Both of Abe's eyebrows went up. What embarrassing thing was Leo up to? Because of course that's what it would be. Something extremely subtle, yet all the same meant to embarrass the crap out of him.

"Fun?" he said with a grin, desperately attempting to be as subtle as he could. "Fun for whom?"

"Fun for everyone," Leo quipped. And then his best friend paused, looking directly at him. "Even you."

"What do you have up your sleeve, Leo?" Batya asked, her eyes twinkling chocolate drops. "I am dying to find out."

"So," Leo said, apparently having decided that he'd been egged on enough, ushering them into the kitchen, "I've been watching some of the lectures, and I have to say I've been fascinated."

"Really?" Sarah asked. It sounded like he'd impressed her.

"*He* keeps yelling at me about spices and international food."

Abe shook his head. "I do. I have. Because…"

"Anyway," Leo continued as if he hadn't said a word, which also was par for the course with them. "One day, I discovered—and how it took me this long to discover this is my fault—that apparently Italy has one of the oldest Jewish communities. And their Hanukkah food is fun and some say the reason we fry vegetables."

Sarah's eyes lit up. "Oh woooooooow."

Huge surprise.

Practical joke or surprise party Abe wasn't sure, but Leo was sure proud of himself. "I don't know whether to yell at you or praise you," Abe finally said.

"I'm not Artur," Leo replied with a laugh. "So I'm not making that choice for you. You're going to have to do it on your own."

Abe nodded as Batya beamed next to him.

"So," Batya asked, inquisitiveness in her eyes. He loved to watch her when she was like this, loved to see her exhibit the signs of the television host she would become. "We're having Italian Hanukkah food tonight?"

Leo nodded. "Exactly. Just because I couldn't be at the lectures doesn't mean I wasn't inspired by them."

Yep. Leo was in his element, and Sarah was clearly about twelve feet off the ground.

Not to mention the expression on Batya's face. Joyful, but the kind of joy that came from the most unexpected of possibilities, the idea that what she'd done would expand someone's horizons.

She was always gorgeous, but now?

This was a masterpiece.

"Thank you," Batya said, as she squeezed his hand.

And as they sat down at the table, the smells overcame them. "Pollo fritto, fried eggplant pieces, and mashed potato latkes, which are the custom. And for dessert, I give you

Fritelli de Chanukah."

"I can't believe this," Sarah said. "Do you want to do a special for the festival? Maybe have people get tickets for a tasting?"

And as Leo and Sarah worked out the details, Abe turned to Batya, basking in the glow of her cheeks. He wanted to make sure she realized the kind of connections she was making. How important what she'd done actually was, and how the impact of creating conversations about Jewish food would be felt beyond the Rivertown High School auditorium.

Of course, then there was Leo. His best friend. Who'd managed to impress Sarah enough to get a slot at the Hanukkah festival, bolster Batya's confidence, and make him feel at home. Again. "Leo," Abe said with a laugh, "you sly fish."

"Support," Leo replied with a wink. "Allyship is a verb, you know."

"Neighbor is a good noun," Sarah added. "I haven't eaten fried chicken this good in a long time. And the latkes?"

"I don't miss the applesauce or sour cream debate," Abe found himself saying. "Not at all."

"Too much swaying by the lemon and nutmeg on the chicken. My God, this is good," Isaac said, an unreserved statement of admiration Abe hadn't been sure the man was actually capable of.

"If you're this excited about the chicken," Leo quipped as

he put the next round of plates on the table, "I can't wait to see what you think about the latkes."

"Or," Abe quipped, "the fritelli."

And of all the things in the world, Abe found himself wondering which was sweeter—being able to spend time with Batya and her friends like this or the fritelli itself. He was looking forward to finding out.

⟫⟫⟩✦⟨⟨⟨

WHEN DINNER WAS over, Batya almost regretted the fact that she'd driven herself. As her friends headed out, she was left with Abe in the parking lot.

"The competition starts Saturday night," she said.

"I am aware of that." He smiled. "So…"

"Maybe it's better to not see each other in person until after the competition."

He nodded. "No appearance of impropriety. Don't want to make it look weird."

"Exactly."

He was agreeing way too easily. What was going on? Why was he so calm about…?

"What are your rules about ice cream?" Abe asked.

"What do you mean?"

"Smoke signals? You know the wood I use has a really good visual spread distance."

"I'm not following."

He stepped closer. "Text messages? Voicemails? Video chats?"

"Wouldn't that defeat the purpose?"

"So there's a line. Okay, No real-time video chats. I can live with that. What about those ice cream deliveries?"

He stepped closer, put his arm around her.

"I'm not sure." She leaned into him, as if the world was shifting. "Why ice cream?"

"Well," he said with a smile. "You're not a sour cream fan with your latkes. Which means dairy is safe territory. Which means a dairy dessert that is not fried is even safer." He leaned so close, she could feel his breath on her neck, the taste of sugar syrup and the fritelli Leo had spent hours making. "And a dairy dessert that is not fried that I didn't have a hand in making is the safest of all."

She looked up and met his eyes. Gorgeous, green, sparkling. "And what if I don't want safe?"

"That goes back to video conversations, which you've already told me is unsafe."

"I said it wouldn't be a good idea. Not that it would be unsafe. So. Text messages, emails, letters, smoke signals. All indirect methods of conversation. And ice cream if you so choose."

"Burn the evidence?"

"Delete," she said, feeling bold, letting her fingers dive deeply into his hair. "Destroy."

"So," he said with a smile, "how do we seal this bargain?"

"With a kiss, of course. As long as you approve."

"Oh," he said, his voice breathless to her ears. "I absolutely approve. Kiss me."

And without reason, without pause, without further thought, she leaned in closer and pressed her lips to his and lost her mind, let it go as she let the sensation of him, his scent, his skin on hers—

"No kissing in the parking lot."

"Love you too, Leo," Abe said as he broke the kiss, laughing as he put his forehead against hers.

"Now go home, you crazy kids," Leo said with a smile. "Talk to you two soon."

As Leo went inside, Batya kissed Abe's forehead. "We'll talk?"

He nodded. "We'll talk. After, right?"

"Definitely after."

But as she watched him walk away, she wished later was, in fact, much, much sooner.

Chapter Nineteen

THE NIGHT OF the competition, Batya was ready—at least as ready as she was going to be. Once George had fully thrown his support behind her, Linda had as well. She'd been absolutely wonderful, genuine, and so very helpful as Batya made her way through the production meetings, the screen tests, and the storyboard moments.

She was even getting better at dealing with her stage fright, reminding herself that this whole process of television was tech, and that there was very little tech she couldn't fix. Going through the mental process of dealing with each potential problem before she got onstage also helped. Much more than she expected.

"He likes your site, and your ideas," Linda had said.

"Thank you," she said, smiling. It was much better than gushing, which was, in fact, what she wanted to do.

"So," Linda continued, as if she hadn't noticed the complete flash of adoration. "Night one is kosher-meat themed, and thank you for the clip. We're going to start the night with the Goldberg quote from lecture four about kosher meat, and then—"

"One hour for preparation, right?"

Linda nodded. "Now you go to makeup and then outside in front of everybody."

Batya nodded. "Got it."

She was ready.

At least she was as ready as she could be.

"Break a leg. George is pulling for you."

Batya headed down the hall toward the space they'd set up for hair and makeup. She went through her lines in her head as the stylist washed and flattened her hair. One hour to prep.

"Ten minutes!"

Batya nodded as the makeup artist did her thing. "Right. Ten minutes."

She swallowed, and then when she was ready, smiled. "Thank you. I very much appreciate it."

"George is pulling for you," the makeup artist said as she smiled back.

As Batya headed outside, into the Rivertown square where the first night of competition was taking place, her hands weren't shaking, there wasn't sweat running down the back of her neck. Nothing like she'd been before.

Which was when she realized that she could make George and Rivertown, and maybe Abe, proud of her. All in one fell swoop.

ABE STOOD IN the Rivertown Square with all of the other contestants. Everybody was keeping to themselves.

It was cold of course; December in Rivertown never really was anything else. And his hands were shaking, sweaty. The only reason he wasn't completely losing his mind was that Artur had agreed to be his sous chef.

"You're going to win," Artur informed him under his breath. "You're going to do this."

Abe wished he could believe his friend, but he could only breathe easier when Batya emerged onto the stage. She was beautiful, ready to take this competition and make it hers.

"Think about what she'll think of your entry after tonight is done."

Abe laughed. "Really, huh?"

"Anything to get those mitts of yours to stop shaking."

But the moment they pressed play on the recording and the sound of Aaron Goldberg's voice washed over him, he found himself in a state of icy calm.

"It's important," the older man said, "to treat kosher meat well. To apply spices and let it sing, to desalinate and make it beautiful."

"And so," Batya said, turning to the crowd, excitement in her eyes, "chefs, you have one hour to put together latkes that take the flavor of the kosher meat we love. Your time," she said, her voice clear and strong "begins now."

Abe pulled out his cooler and the wood chips he'd brought. He prepped them before turning to the potatoes.

He pulled out aluminum foil and placed the potatoes in the foil after washing and peeling them.

"You're smoking them?"

"I need my sauce," he said as he turned to Artur. "Stir as if your life depended on it." He pulled out his phone and went to his notes app, searching for the recipe he'd added the night before. "Here," he said, as he passed Artur his phone after finding the recipe. "This is it."

Artur saluted and went to work, gathering everything according to instructions as Abe shoved his potatoes in the oven.

Next, he diced the onions, chopping fast.

Apples came next. Artur gave him the newly made sauce, and Abe poured it into his food processor with the apples.

"Barbecue applesauce?"

Abe nodded again. He was in prep mode. "To my advantage. Eggs, please."

As Artur cracked eggs, Abe pulled out the bags he used with the wood chips, placing them inside the oven. The goal was to create smoke, not burn the place down, and give the potatoes and the latkes the same smoky flavor his barbecue had.

Eggs went into the bowl, and then his favorite matzo meal. As the timer went off, he opened the door to the oven and pulled out the chips and the potatoes, opening the aluminum jackets and taking a deep whiff to discover the potatoes had caught the hickory scent.

"Nailed it," he said, taking a few minutes of precious time to pump his fist.

The wide-eyed, bright expression on Artur's face said it all.

But Abe couldn't stop to think about this, because the potatoes needed to go into the second food processor, the one he'd brought from home. The smoky scent of hickory released by the potatoes as the food processor did its work, transported him to busy Saturdays in his kitchen and his backyard, far away from the chilly outdoor setup in the center of town. Finally, the potatoes were sufficiently grated so he shut down the processor, poured the grated potatoes into the bowl, and mixed it all together.

Then he went to the stove. Pan. Oil. A basic safflower oil did the trick for this. The oil wasn't going to get the chance to overwhelm the smoked potatoes. He tried not to stare at the clock as he willed the oil to heat.

Finally the drops of water he'd put in the oil started to sizzle. It was ready.

Without thinking, he grabbed the ice cream scoop from the drawer, washed it off, and started to scoop out the latke mix from the bowl.

Three judges. Three plates plus his test two. Full batch.

His heart pounded, willing the oil to do its job and prepare those latkes.

"Plates?"

Abe nodded. "Yes. How's the sauce?'

"Amazing," Artur replied. "Perfect balance."

The sauce went on the plates, and as he took the latkes off the heat, he put them quickly on a paper towel to get off some of the excess oil before moving them on to the plates.

And then he heard Batya's voice. "Your cooking time is done."

Triumphantly, feeling the slight wave of exhaustion and exhilaration from the coming crash that would surely hit him later, he raised his arms and smacked the hand Artur extended in his direction.

"We did it," he said.

"No," Artur replied with a grin as he reached for a towel to wipe his forehead. "You did it. I just came along to help you."

Which he'd remember for the rest of his life. But now he had to face the judges. By himself.

He hoped he was ready.

BATYA WASN'T SUPPOSED to be involved or feel anything other than neutral as the host. The forced neutrality was especially going to drive her batty as she sat off stage, watching Dr. Engleman guide the section of the night where the contestants presented their food to the judges. Just like people who watched various cooking competitions at home, she couldn't help but get involved in some way emotionally with each candidate and their journey. What brought them here, what led them to cook the way they did, and how?

Finally, it was Abe's turn. The one she was the most emotionally un-neutral with.

Beyond all reason she hoped the judges liked what he brought to the table. Literally.

"Hi," he said. "Abe Newman. I grew up in this town, came back three years ago to, oddly enough, spend more time on my barbecue pop-up. And so that's the direction I went. I didn't just tie my sauce to the applesauce, but I also smoked the potatoes with my wood chips, just to get a basic smoke on them. These latkes are center stage enough, but I wanted to give them a bit of a smoky flavor to tie in with the barbecue sauce." He laughed. "I brought my favorite wood chips as a lucky charm, but I didn't expect to use them. They're hickory and cherry wood, by the way."

That was the most difficult part of this, the long wait between his introduction and the hand-off to Dr. Engleman. How would the judges react to smoked potato latkes and apple barbecue sauce?

"Thank you, chef," Dr. Engleman said.

"And now we wait for the judges and their opinions."

She couldn't help but hope for the best, and the best was Abe making it through to the second round.

THE RUSH, THE energy that came from the fact he'd made it past the first round of competition made Abe feel like he'd gotten onto a hot air balloon. He had to wait, of course, till the night was over to chat with Batya, but it was worth it to see the excitement in her eyes.

When he found her, by the part of the high school that exited right onto the parking lot, he beamed. He couldn't help himself, and, frankly, he didn't want to.

"You made it," she said, grinning.

"Who knew that my smoking skills would come in handy making latkes?"

She laughed. "You never know what might come in handy."

"True," he said. "Very true." He paused, looked around. "You have plans for the night?"

"Actually," she said, "I do. I have an engagement party to go to."

He raised an eyebrow. "Engagement?"

She nodded. "Yeah. Sarah and Isaac. She wanted a wedding by the menorah, so he popped the question right in front of it."

"Very cool. And the party?"

"Carol, Sarah's boss at the bookstore, organized it. I think there might be a lot of Hanukkah there."

He snorted. "I could see there'd be Hanukkah there. So I guess I'll see you tomorrow then? Tell them I said congratulations."

She didn't respond immediately, but she responded, although he could barely hear her. "What?"

He could see the nerves in her eyes. In the way she let his hand go. "Do…um, do you want to come with me?"

He smiled. Casual. Casual. He had to be casual. This was big.

"Could be fun. Interesting latkes, good group of people. Why not? Good way to celebrate."

She nodded. "Good deal. So, do you want me to drive and we'll leave your car here?"

"Sounds like a plan," he said.

She'd taken a leap, and he figured he might as well jump with her. "Or," he ventured, "you can follow me to my place and we can drop my car off."

"That works." She paused. "You're on the way to Hollowville, right?"

He nodded. He wanted this whole thing to be as painless as possible. "I'm closer," he said.

"Makes sense," she said.

Was it relief in her voice? Nerves? Surprise?

At this point, as he got into his car and punched on the music, it really didn't matter. He was going with Batya to an engagement party in Hollowville. And he couldn't wait to get there.

WHEN BATYA PARKED the car in front of Tante Shelly's apartment, she wasn't sure what to do with herself. And if she was going to be honest, this was a bigger case of nerves than hosting the latke fry-off had put into her stomach.

Oh. Dear. God.

She was bringing Abe to Sarah's *engagement party*.

In Hollowville.

Yes, they'd talked about spending time with her Hollowville friends, but in her mind that meant dinner and maybe a movie with either Isaac and Sarah or Jacob and Anna. Calm, low-key conversation over whatever.

Not a huge party where the entire town of Hollowville was going to be in attendance.

Oh God.

Which meant *everybody* was going to ask her questions about who he was and what he meant to her, and Anna and Sarah would never let her live it down.

She had debated calling ahead, warning *someone*, probably Anna, that she was bringing Abe to this party before she'd pulled into his driveway and invited him into her car, not as a date but as…

Oh hell.

"You sure it's okay?"

"It's fine," she said as they got out of the car. "Really. It's just fine."

She could see the doubt in his eyes, not that serious doubt that usually meant trouble, but the doubt that usually came before some kind of joke. But this time, he offered his arm, and as she took it, he leaned over and placed a soft kiss on her temple.

This was a date.

This was actually, really, completely a date.

She swallowed.

"You made it through hosting a cooking competition," he said with a laugh. "This can't be that bad."

She sighed, leaned into him a little bit. "Imagine if I weren't quiz bowl friendly. And what meeting our group would be like."

Abe nodded immediately. "I'll be on my best behavior. Unless you don't want me to behave."

She snorted as they approached the bookstore. "I just want you to be you," she said. "That's all I want."

His smile was easy and just perfect. "Then that, my lady, is what I will do."

Of course, that was when Carol spied them, hanging outside the threshold. Yentas were everywhere, she decided.

"Come in, come in," the older woman said, beaming as she opened the door.

Abe took Batya's hand, and as she got a glimpse of the inside, she stopped in her tracks. The store had been turned into an open space, the lights and the bright music and the eight menorahs that sat all over the room.

"Welcome to Hanukkah," Anna said as she came over. And then she turned toward Abe. "I see," she said.

Batya's decision not to call Anna in advance had clearly been a mistake. "Can you not?" Batya said with a laugh.

Abe shook his head; she was lucky that he was that easygoing about this. "I don't mind."

Which was, she decided, true for the moment, except his calm exterior lasted until someone turned the music on.

And suddenly, the room was dancing to a song that described the process of making latkes.

Abe burst out laughing and took her hand. "A dance, my lady?"

She grinned back at him and let him lead her onto the dance floor.

"Too on the nose?" he asked.

"Very, very perfect for the person who this party is for. Fascinatingly amusing for us. Unless there is a DJ on the job."

"And if there is?"

"I'd say that someone is making a joke of this."

He stopped for a second. "This?"

"We're here. Someone noticed that I arrived and not alone," she said, putting her arm around him. "I'm with someone who is competing in a latke-fry off. Where one needs a latke recipe."

Abe nodded. "Or it could only mean that someone is just randomly letting a playlist do its thing?"

Batya laughed. "Not with this crew."

"We don't spend time with people who aren't aware of

the details, huh?"

She shook her head. "Noope. Not us."

"Never," he said with a laugh. "Never."

Of course never would she have believed that not only was she on a date with Abe but she'd also managed to merge her Rivertown past—and present?—with her Hollowville present. Stranger things had happened, but she'd chalk this one up to a Hanukkah miracle.

DESPITE THE PRESSURE of the situation, being Batya's date to the engagement party of friends who mattered to her, Abe was actually enjoying himself. The party was fun; he'd talked to a few people, had himself a drink and some of the food. It was dairy, and he could tell it was made by a master, which was even more obvious when he saw Chana milling around and chatting in the center of the crowd.

But despite all of that, he couldn't help but be in awe of Batya. She was gorgeous, like a shining, bubbly star in the middle of this group of people she was so amazingly comfortable with.

He wanted her to be comfortable with him too, wanted to spend time with her and not worry that at any moment, the sword of Damocles attached to an event that had defined their past would drop and break their present. Which meant he couldn't wait any longer to talk to her, and tell her how he felt. What he'd *always* felt.

Determined, if nothing else just to see her and spend more time with her, he headed toward the dance floor where she was dancing with a few of her friends. Her face brightened when she saw him, and she moved just a bit to let him in. He took her hands, and she continued to sway along with him to the bright beat of the music.

As they danced, Abe found himself thinking about the lyrics, that the perfect night meant more than just the perfect night. It was the people, the person he was with that made everything perfect. He couldn't wait.

"Can I talk to you?"

He felt her hold on him tighten. Nerves? Fears?

He wasn't sure; all he knew was that he needed to get it out in the open and deal with this before it crushed them.

"Sounds serious," she said, in a way that made him think she was trying to be casual when she just wasn't. "Is it? Should I worry?"

The boulder and the seed, or whatever allusion Artur had referred to. She saw it as a boulder; of course she'd be worried about things he'd say. And so he smiled. "No. Not really."

She raised an eyebrow, skepticism pouring out of her, but all the same let him lead her toward the back of the store, one of the few places where there were chairs, where tiny tea lights illuminated the spaces where menorahs weren't.

They sat down, and he took her hand. "I assume this

isn't a proposal?"

He shook his head. "No. It's not. But," he said, "there's something I want to say to you."

"You said," she said. "So here we are."

"Fortunately, I'm not an eighteen-year-old kid who had his first taste of alcohol that wasn't served at a Passover seder. I'm an adult, who understands what he feels and…"

She was frozen, stock-still. Her jaw dropped, her eyes wide.

She shook her head and took his hand, leading him outside, out to the back parking lot, in the cold, away from everything.

Once they'd settled, amidst the dumpsters behind the store and the empty parking spaces dotted with random trash, she glared at him.

"What. The. Hell?"

"Just let me say this," he said, grabbing for words, any of them, that would stop this train from rolling off the tracks. He'd caught her by surprise and he'd meant to be gentler about this.

Instead of being gentle or careful, he'd gotten caught up in the moment, and forgotten how important it was to ease her into a conversation like this one, to prepare for it. And now he had to make the bed he was going to lie in. He wasn't going to get another chance if he messed this up.

"I know this isn't the right time or place, and I know I should have thought of that before I said anything. But please. Let me say this."

She let his hand go, folded her arms, and stared at him. She didn't want to listen, that was obvious; she wanted to be inside celebrating her friend's engagement.

Heck, so did he.

Unfortunately, the die had been cast and this was the moment. Not over breakfast or brunch or in a soft comfortable place like she probably would have wanted. He and Batya were going to have the most serious conversation of their lives to this point in front of dumpsters, behind Hollowville's town bookstore.

He sighed, having no other option, pulled the words together. "Back in high school. At the party. I'd had my first beer. Two, three. Everybody has different reactions to alcohol. Mine…well, I was slurring and I couldn't get words out properly. So it sounded like I didn't feel the same. But I was desperately trying to say I did. I messed up the words and I messed up things with you. And I'm sorry."

He didn't want to look at her, didn't want to see the expression in her eyes. The fact there was a long pause was a good sign, right?

"Is that why you don't drink that much?"

Abe nodded looking up at her, meeting the calm in her brown eyes. "Yeah. Pretty much. Being the cook helps too."

The silence that followed wasn't a bad one but an easy one. One where, against all odds he could make, she stepped toward him, took his hand. "I understand. And I didn't realize."

Abe nodded, and the relief gushed out of him as if he were Old Faithful. "Thank you," he said. "I know this wasn't the best place to talk about this, and I know I sprung it on you."

"It's fine," she said with a small smile. "We were going to have to deal with the sucking wound between us at some point."

Abe nodded, and he was glad she was smiling. This was harder than he'd expected and yet had gone so much better than he could have ever dreamed. "Yeah. That sucking one. The one I inflicted."

"You mean the wound inflicted by an eighteen-year-old kid who shouldn't have been drinking on a seventeen-year-old kid who probably should have?"

He laughed. "I don't know about that, but maybe."

"We're older. We're wiser," she said, putting an arm around his shoulder. "I think it's okay. You're also a really good kisser."

"There is that to recommend me. And I do know my way around a latke recipe." He paused. "Do you want to go to the festival tomorrow with me? You know, meander the food court?"

"I wish I could," she said. "But I have too much to deal with for the fry-off. I'm going the day after the competition. I promised Sarah I would." She paused, bit her lip. "Do you want to come with me?"

"I'd love to."

"And we'll celebrate our achievements together, just as intended."

"Hmm?"

"Running around in ridiculous Hanukkah hats," he said as he ran a hand through her hair. "Eating latkes and all of those things."

The look in her eyes was so bright and so excited, he couldn't stand it. He was happy. Happier than he'd been in a really long time.

"I love it."

And thankfully, he was smart enough not to say he loved her.

Not yet.

Chapter Twenty

THE NEXT NIGHT, as filming went into the town theatre for the second round, Abe was warm. He didn't have to expect adrenaline to deal with his body temperature. It was all the theatre.

He was also alone; no sous chefs for the second round.

Which meant as he stood in his spot, he was the only one to listen to his nerves, his fears and the ridiculous ways he was trying to get his hands to stop shaking and sweating.

Cooking latkes with shaking and sweaty hands was going to be impossible.

"Hello, everybody."

A familiar voice came through the speakers, and Abe went from nervous to angry in point five seconds. He was going to kill Leo, for no other reason than because he was here. On the stage.

"My name is Leo Fratelli, and I'm from Fratelli's restaurant in Rivertown. What you may not know is that Italy has a thriving Jewish community, and though I'm not a member of that community, I've found their food traditions fascinating and wonderful. Tonight, I'd like to tell you about the ricotta latke."

Leo stepped away, and Abe pulled himself together.

He could do this.

The scoop, the food processor.

Applesauce, contrast the flavors. Not sour cream.

Ricotta.

"Chefs," Batya said as she came to the center of the stage, taking the microphone, "you have one hour to duplicate the famous and sometimes controversial ricotta latke. May…may…may…"

His heart stopped. If he could, he'd go up there and encourage Batya as she stumbled. All he could do was attempt to mentally push her over this moment.

"May your own creations be less controversial and just as tasty as this latke. Your time starts now."

He nodded, relieved more for her than worried for his ability to tackle this thing. But he had to press on. He set up the two food processors and removed the recipe from the box.

Ricotta, eggs, sugar? He shrugged. Okay.

Matzo meal, baking powder.

The food processor ran with the ingredients for the latke as he tried to think of what he could do to work with the dipping sauce. How could he make it work?

Lemon. Lemon worked really well with ricotta. Maybe he could put lemon zest in the homemade applesauce?

Yes. That would work.

Now he was set.

Oil in the frying pan.

Out came the ice cream scoop.

Once again, he quickly chopped apples and threw them into the second food processor as he waited for the oil to heat up sufficiently.

As the pan got itself together, he scooped the latke mixture from the first food processor and put the scoops of batter in the pan with the oil. Three judges. One test.

He blew out a breath.

Once the apples had reached the right consistency, he stopped the food processor and poured the mixture into a mixing bowl. This time, he added a bit of lemon zest, and stirred. A careful taste test proved his point.

A peek at his latkes showed they were browning and gorgeous.

Phew.

And when it was time to lift them out of the pan, they were perfect. His test was perfect. They sat easily on the plates. On top of the applesauce.

"Chefs," Batya said. "Your time is up."

He was done. He'd navigated this difficult recipe, somehow. He didn't feel triumphant; he just felt done. Tired. But winning chefs sometimes had bad nights, right?

But if he were honest with himself, he was prouder of Batya, who'd managed to get through that difficult moment on stage, than of his moment by himself in the kitchen.

ONCE AGAIN BATYA waited nervously as all the chefs made their way through the conversations with the judges. Once again, she tried not to get excited as Abe's turn approached.

"Hello, everybody" he said as he approached the judges. "Applesauce with a bit of lemon zest."

"Why not sour cream?"

She bit her nails. Held her breath.

"The applesauce is a good contrast to the ricotta in the latkes. I figured dipping ricotta in sour cream would be too much. When you dip cheese blintzes in sour cream, you end up with conflicting cheese flavors."

"It makes sense," said the judge. "I like the fact that you thought about the way the flavors go together."

Thankfully, Abe not only had an answer, but it was also an answer the judges seemed to appreciate.

But as the first judge cut into his latke, it fell apart, as if it were gushing cheese lava on the plate.

"Your latke browned before it could cook sufficiently," the first judge said.

So did the second.

Her heart pounded against her chest. This moment, sitting right here was almost as bad as when she messed up on stage. But she got through that moment, mostly because she saw him, the way he didn't take his eyes off her, as if he was sending her encouragement from the competition area.

All she hoped was that the energy she sent him from here was as helpful.

"This tastes absolutely horrible," said another judge.

What she'd done hadn't worked. The worst had happened.

It didn't take long for the judges to confer and deliver the verdict.

"Abraham Newman, I'm sorry to tell you, that you have been eliminated."

Her heart went right into her stomach. She needed to find him immediately. He was going to be a wreck. And that hurt more than everybody seeing her completely mess up during that first segment.

➤➤➤✕◀◀◀

DR. ENGLEMAN'S WORDS hit Abe's chest like a frying pan. The spoon scooped his heart right out and put it into a fire. He had to hold himself together, completely and fully. He couldn't let on how awful he felt. He couldn't let on how disappointed he was.

His dream was over.

He was an accountant who made barbecue on the weekend, not an aspiring chef. Cooking was for leisure and for fun, not for him.

In the chaos of the elimination, he smiled and went in search of Batya. "So," he told her, "I gotta go. Tomorrow's going to be an early day, and the office is going to be wild. I'll call you from the train, see how you're doing, okay?"

The expression on her face was the human emoji of what he was feeling inside. "You're leaving?"

He nodded. He had to keep it casual, otherwise he'd lose it completely, not only in front of her but in front of everybody. "Yeah. Time to pack the old lunch, grab the briefcase, and go back to the world of numbers and accounting. The restaurant life isn't for me."

"This isn't you," she said. And then she paused. "Come here."

He needed to leave; it was going to be 5:30 in the morning really quickly, and the train he needed to take to the city didn't wait for anybody, let alone him.

But because he would do anything for her, he let her wrap her hand around his, let her take him to the little backstage nook they'd found for other reasons. "Look," she said. "I hate that you're eliminated. Honestly, whoever decided that ricotta latkes were the thing you'd have to duplicate wasn't...whatever. Anyway, you can't give up."

"They were smart," he told her. "Separated the good from the bad. The wheat from the chaff. Me from the rest of the field."

"You need to try. You need to stay."

"For what reason? I got eliminated, Batya."

"You can still talk to Chana or Moshe or even Aaron Goldberg."

"They don't want to talk to someone who can't make latkes on national television."

"Forget the complex ridiculous ricotta latkes. These people? They *like* you. They want you to succeed." She bit her lip. "I do, too."

Abe shook his head, tried to ignore the pain he could see in her eyes. "So you only want me when I'm successful, is that it? You only want me when I'm chasing dreams? I'm not enough for you when I'm doing what's best for me?"

"Who says going back to your old job is best for you? Who says doing things that will destroy you from the inside is best for you? Not me."

"You're still standing, you're here. You overcame your fears. And I'm thrilled. But that's not my path."

"You need to dream. Dreaming is what we do, what we should do. We make our own luck."

"How do you know about luck? How do you know about choices?" That hit hard, he knew, and, dear God, he wanted to take it back. But it was too late now.

"I know the choices I made," she said, looking like she was holding herself together by a thread. "The things that happened to me? They make me better, give me fuel to live a better life. I know that."

"How?" And then the words he was thinking blew out of his mouth before he could even stop them. "You've *never* been satisfied with life. You've never been fulfilled enough to stay in one place. And that's the problem."

That was when he ended the conversation and left before he could cause any more damage to anybody else, including her. He didn't go through the front, but through the secret exit that everybody who'd spent any time there knew about. The back door, through the semi-secret hallway that took him to the parking lot. The one that kept him focused, got him to his car, and got him home without anybody knowing where he'd gone.

IT TOOK MUCH longer for Batya to calm herself down than she'd expected. In fact, it took another trip to the makeup station to fix the mascara she'd cried off. She eventually emerged from the side as Dr. Engleman approached the crowd. There had been a commotion, of course.

"Everything okay?"

Other than the rather cavernous hole inside of her, everything was perfect. But the show had to go on; her complete and utter collapse would happen later. Which meant she had to pretend, like she had way too often, that what happened didn't matter. "Yes," she said, as if she was also convincing herself. "It's fine. How much time do we have left?"

"We've got one more segment to film."

"How's the audience?"

Audience. Like they were random people she didn't know, as opposed to people she knew from synagogue, her

Hollowville friends, even the camera crew she'd gotten to know over the last few days.

They were good people.

"So," Dr. Engleman said, reaching into his pocket and pulling out a bright blue envelope. "Mr. Gold has left us with one of his special gold challenges, and he specified that this is the time he would like us to read it. Would you like to do the honors, Batya, or would you like me to?"

As the audience, as Rivertown, cheered, she found herself smiling. "You take it, Dr. Engleman, because you're who this amazing crowd really wants to see."

Her former teacher smiled. "All righty then." He opened the envelope. "Our Gold's challenge for this event is a people's choice. One candidate who was eliminated tonight will be brought back for tomorrow's event because of you, those who are here, watching in the audience. Who is your favorite competitor who lost their way but deserves to bring their special style of latke cooking to the fry-off tomorrow? Who will the people choose as their champion?"

And without a pause, without surprise the chant began. "Abe. Abe." It started in the corner, and like a wave, moved to slowly cover the audience. It gained life and noise and finally, Dr. Engleman grinned. "And we have our answer. Rivertown's own Abe Newman will get the chance to join us tomorrow, here, at the finals."

So many thoughts ran through her head. Exhilaration, excitement. And then the nervous, heart-stopping thought.

How the heck was she going to get Abe to come back?

Chapter Twenty-One

THE NEXT MORNING, Abe woke up to multiple messages on his phone and multiple emails, all of which he ignored.

He made himself coffee, turned on the Meal Network for a split second before switching to his favorite news channel, catching a few highlights from Sophie Katz's show the night before, and then turning it to the business channel.

After a quick, basic breakfast, he packed his lunch, grabbed the book he'd been trying to read, his headphones, and drove to the train station. He stopped to buy a ticket because his train pass had expired.

Back to the same train ride, the brilliant Hudson shining in the window, the same subway ride that took him from the train station down to the Financial District and its sleek buildings and cobblestoned streets.

This was where he belonged.

He waved to the security guard, passed his ID over at the desk, and got on the elevator with the wood paneling he'd never been able to decipher.

When he arrived at his floor, the floor of the firm where

he'd spent most of his professional life, he greeted the receptionist, ignored the signs of the holidays; the way the entranceway was decorated in red, green, blue and gold, and headed to his office.

Everything was just as he'd left it: the pen his grandfather had given him on graduation from business school, the advanced business degree in taxation, and the various accounting certificates.

He settled his book and his coffee on top of his desk and prepared to dive into the email.

Same password that he'd always had, same wait time it always took his dinosaur of a computer to start up. He almost missed the moments where he stood over the kitchen sink in his house back in Rivertown looking over this email.

Almost.

And then the important email that would start the course of his day arrived. HM Tax update.

Which was a thing and a half to understand; this was… No. Had been his friend.

He shoved those ridiculous emotions aside and read the email. Joint filing for next year. Preparations, it said.

Yes. There was going to be a wedding.

Batya…

No.

He read through the email only to discover that Jacob's fiancée had a minimum of seven 1099s.

He blinked. He sent a quick message to Frazier, the intermediary partner who was taking over partial responsibility for the taxes.

He took a sip of his coffee as he waited for a reply. It was going to take a lot of restructuring to pull this off.

To: ANewman@LiebWaxmanTax.com
From: JFrazier@LiebWaxmanTax.com

Mr. Lieb is contacting the client. Hold steady.

He swallowed. Okay. It couldn't be so bad. Could it?

BATYA PACED THE space of her parents' house. And swallowed another sip of her coffee.

She wasn't alone. Artur, Claire, Leo, Anna, and Jacob were there with her. She could do this.

She'd called them when all she got was Abe's voicemail.

And that was the only thing she could do. Linda had heard their conversation the night before.

You're a local. It's understandable that you're going to have relationships with some of the competitors. We get that. But that conversation between you and Mr. Newman? If any of the microphones were recording, that could have been a disaster. Any clips of the conversation surface and any possible impartiality you might have? Gone.

Which means if there are any signs or hints that you're in any way involved with him before the competition is over, you're done.

Batya couldn't give up her chance. Even when she desperately wanted Abe to take advantage of his opportunities, too.

"No luck," Artur said, swearing again as he dropped his phone on the table. "He's a stubborn sonofabitch."

"Sarah said she's coming for lunch if she can get away," Anna said as she looked at her phone.

"Sarah can't get away," Batya said. "Festival day. She's not going anywhere, and Isaac is coming up tonight to help."

Anna looked back down at her phone. "She said it's an emergency, so she'll be here."

Claire smiled. "It's an emergency. Friend-related."

Anna nodded. "Anyway, we're glad to be here. For you."

The distinct sound of a phone rang. Everybody picked theirs up. This time, Jacob was the one who swore.

"It's mine," he said. "It's the tax firm. Hold on."

Batya tried not to get too excited as Jacob answered the call. Abe had mentioned he was doing Jacob's taxes, and if the tax firm was calling Jacob, it was entirely possible Abe had gone in to work.

Which meant it was entirely possible that Abe could be found. And convinced to come back and take the chance he deserved, the one he needed.

"Tell him I'm on my way," Jacob said in very even, very measured tones. As if he were used to his wishes being taken into account immediately. "Tell him I want to talk to him.

This is a delicate situation, and I need to speak to him face-to-face. Thank you."

A chill ran across the back of her neck when he stopped speaking, when she looked into his eyes.

Was Abe okay?

Batya's heart pounded against her chest.

Please.

She didn't want to ask, but Jacob smiled.

"We got him," he said. "He's at the office. I'll go and get him."

Artur and Leo looked up. "There's a 3:10 p.m. train," Leo said, picking up the train schedule they'd put on the table.

Jacob threw his head back in what Batya could only interpret as an exaggerated bit of impatience. "What is with this system?" he said already getting to his feet. "I can't wait that long. I'm going to drive."

"You hate traffic," Anna pointed out.

"I'll deal with it for this," he said, reaching out to touch her cheek with his knuckles. Anna leaned in for a quick kiss. For a second Batya was jealous of the now easy, but hard-fought companionship that tied them together. "Tell Sarah I'll pick up Isaac on the way," he said, his arm around Anna. "Tell him he needs to find somewhere in Manhattan because I am not going to Brooklyn to drive back here."

When he turned to Batya, she could see the steel in his eyes; it was obvious why people were intimidated by him when he wanted them to be. But this was different; this was the guy she bonded with over Shadow Squad. This was her friend. "I'll bring him back," he said. "I promise."

She nodded. "I can't go with you. I want to. But can you give me two seconds to do something?"

"Absolutely."

The group waited as she grabbed a pen and wrote Abe a note. A list of priorities, of thoughts, and hopes. Then she folded it up, wrote his name on the front. "Take this."

He took the paper from her hand. "Got it."

And then he grabbed his jacket and headed out the door.

"I'll stall," Artur said. "I'll get into his house and get his stuff, bring it over to the theatre."

"I'll help," Leo said, smiling.

It seemed so perfect. Jacob would collect Abe, Artur and Leo would get his stuff, and then Abe would compete.

All she could hope was that it would work. No matter what any of it did to her heart. As long as Abe was okay, she'd be fine.

Eventually.

ABE WAS SURPRISED at how easy it was to settle back into the rhythm of being a tax accountant, dealing with the numbers and organizing papers. Emails, papers, a random note from his father, and it was shaping up to be a good day.

Except there was something nagging at him.

The competition hadn't just been about him. It was also about Batya.

Her life, her choices. Her career. Her ambitions.

His might be out the window with no chance of getting them back; a Jewish chef who failed to make latkes on television wasn't anybody who should be trusted with a deli after all.

But hers? Hers were still wide open. She was hosting a huge Hanukkah-themed competition, and her website was getting more and more popular. What was a relationship without support? Without one of them having the other's back?

He needed to get to Rivertown and fast.

And then there was a knock on his door.

"Come in."

"The client is here," Mr. Lieb said. "And he wants to talk to you."

Jacob. Who had managed to get himself here from somewhere, between Mr. Lieb's phone call and now.

How exactly? And from where?

"This isn't a request," Lieb said as he walked into the office, clearly misinterpreting his slowness to answer. "Mr. Horowitz-Margareten made it very clear on the phone that he wants to talk to you. The specifics of his fiancée's taxes are a delicate matter, and he insisted that he needs to explain them to you in person."

Abe nodded, a plan slowly forming in the back of his mind. "Okay."

"He's a nice guy," Lieb continued. "Good guy. Going to get married soon."

Abe nodded, as if he hadn't met Jacob's fiancée, hadn't attended her best friend's engagement party with the woman he...loved, the friend who rounded out that trio. "Yeah," he said, trying to pretend the conversation they were having was still about tax preparation. "The question I had was about his future wife's 1099 situation and how he wanted that structured—"

"You can ask her yourself."

Jacob. This was the shark in casual clothing, the man who didn't take no for an answer.

"But I have to be honest with you," Jacob continued, as if there weren't even a possibility of an obstacle being put in his way. "We need to talk about opportunities I want to make sure you're aware of. Details, you know."

"I'm interested in talking about details," Abe replied, half paying attention to Jacob, half paying attention to how quickly his boss was walking out of the office. "But first, I have a question to ask you."

Jacob nodded, the shark gone as soon as the door closed. "Talk to me. What's going on?"

"How did you get here?"

"I drove," he said, as if the answer was obvious. "From Rivertown."

"If I told you that I needed to get back to Rivertown as fast as possible, what would you say?"

"I'd say you're saving me some words, my friend. I'd also tell you that I have to make a stop along the way. Which means," Jacob replied, as if he'd scripted the whole thing, "we're going to have time to talk."

And despite everything, Abe realized that this was a conversation he was looking forward to.

AFTER JACOB, LEO, and Artur left, Anna had followed, once Batya had convinced her friend she'd be fine. She also promised all of them that she'd get in touch with Sarah.

She would be fine, and she'd eventually get in contact with Sarah.

Just like she promised.

Only maybe she realized the promise had simply been a way of getting everybody out, so she could deal.

Except her phone buzzed with a weird text from a 516 area code.

Jacob.

Of course.

Got him. If you haven't, let Sarah know where Isaac should be.

It'll be fine. I promise.

She blew out a breath and forced herself to sit down. She needed to pull herself together and call Sarah.

"That," Sarah said after she heard the details, "is a relief. Except how come I feel there's a catch?"

"Isaac is going to have to go to Manhattan because Jacob refuses to drive to Brooklyn."

Sarah snorted on the other end of the phone. "I see. He's going to be in a mood, but it'll be fine." She paused. "Speaking of moods, how are you doing?"

"I just hope Abe gets back," she said. "Which is weird, but I don't want him to lose his chance."

Sarah sighed. "I want you to be happy, and if this ends up working out with Abe, I will be happy for you. But you know the important thing here."

Batya sat against the chair, trying once again to breathe. "I guess I don't know what you think is important."

"You are on the edge of an amazing opportunity. You will be able to change your life with this show, and I don't want you to throw it away because he's acting like…whatever he's acting."

"But—"

"You need to promise me," Sarah interjected, more forcefully than she'd ever heard her friend in the years they'd known each other, "that no matter *what* Jacob manages to bring back, you will stick to what's important to you. Your future matters."

Batya nodded. "Okay. Abe is going to be okay. And if

Jacob doesn't manage to convince—"

She could hear a deep, deep sigh from Sarah on the other end of the line. "I adore you. I adore Anna. But Anna's unshakable belief in Jacob's ability to convince people to do things is...well..."

Batya nodded. "It's not my concern. It shouldn't be my concern. I need to focus on me. And whatever else happens..."

"Will be later."

Batya smiled. "Yes. Later. I hope."

Sarah ended the call, and Batya felt a little better, a little more focused. Whether or not Abe would be able to compete would be up to him. And she hoped more than anything that he'd be able to make the choice that worked for him.

LEAVING THE OFFICE with Jacob was like getting a free pass; just go with good wishes from Mr. Lieb, through the glass doors and into the elevator, down to the parking garage and toward the black sedan he'd remembered seeing in the parking lot at Leo's, the same one that had pulled up to the Rivertown High parking lot.

"Get in, get comfortable" Jacob said with a laugh. "I told you that we're getting a passenger, so if you want to put something in the trunk, let me know."

And as he opened the door, there were coffee cups, a few

water bottles and…this wasn't a ridiculously expensive inner sanctum where Abe would be afraid to breathe wrong.

"What did you expect?" Jacob asked. "I hate traffic, and the idea of not having coffee or food or whatever in my car is ridiculous. So yeah. Few extra bottles of water aren't going to hurt anyone."

Abe did not mean to laugh, but he did. And if nothing else, he felt comfortable. "Oh, thank God."

"Just be careful of the eject button," Jacob replied as he settled himself into the driver's seat and turned on the ignition.

Abe laughed, but as he was starting to learn, you never knew with Jacob. All you knew was what you had: the rumble of the engine as it started and kicked into life as he pulled out of the parking space and then the garage.

"Here's the thing," Jacob said as they waited for their turn at the gate that separated them from the rest of the city. "We need to figure this out before Isaac gets in the car—did I tell you I hate the fact I have to drive the length of Manhattan to pick him up?"

As they pulled past the gate, there was, of course, traffic.

Predictably, Jacob swore in at least two different languages, one of which might have been Yiddish.

"You didn't, but I would too, considering the mess of vehicles in the city today."

"What makes today any different from any of the other ones, right?"

Abe shook his head and laughed. "And I can give you three other questions to follow." Joking with Jacob was fun, but there were things they had to discuss. More importantly, Abe needed to figure out what mission Jacob thought he was on, who'd sent him. Because the more he thought about it, him showing up now was not a coincidence.

"I have to say," Abe finally said, "I don't know what you're thinking, but this, for me at least, is all about Batya. She's going to host tonight and I need to be there for her, to support her. Even though I'm probably the last person she wants to see right now."

"Open the glove compartment," Jacob said as he changed lanes. "There's something in there for you."

Fair enough. He carefully pressed the button on the front of the glove compartment, opening the door. There was a folded piece of paper in front of him with his name on it, written in Batya's familiar handwriting. He took the paper out of the compartment and closed it.

Abe,

I can't be here now, but if I could be, I would.

I wanted to tell you that I support you, whatever decisions you make. I didn't do that last night and I'm sorry. I hope you're okay no matter what those decisions are, and I'd be honored to stand by your side no matter what happens to me.

Batya

"So," he asked. "You're here because of her?"

"Partially," Jacob replied. "Partially because it was just easier for me to go, and partially because there are some things I wanted to talk to you about."

Abe raised an eyebrow. "What kinds of things? And what exactly does she mean by making decisions?"

"I didn't read the letter, so I'm not sure what she means," Jacob said. "But if you asked me, as your friend, I'd say you're still at a professional crossroads."

He raised an eyebrow. "What professional crossroads are you talking about? I got eliminated from the contest, and I took that as a sign. Same job, same life, same barbecue pop-up on the weekends. That was a life. That was a good life. A safe life."

"But," Jacob continued as he drove through Manhattan. "You're too good to be playing it safe. And you have opportunities knocking."

"I can't just leave Waxman because of a dream that makes no sense, though," Abe said, yanking the conversation back to where it belonged. "You know that. The numbers don't work. *I* can't make that work. Not on my savings, not without a regular income."

"What if I told you that you had a guaranteed income cushion?"

"What do you mean?"

Jacob pulled up to the stoplight, and once again Abe found himself wondering what angle Jacob was playing here.

"I'm thinking of separating the personal taxes from the business side, especially with the complexities associated with next year's joint filing, which means whether you're working with Lieb Waxman or contracting with me directly, you can do either or both of those. Your pick, your choice, my requirement."

What?

"You'd pull your taxes from Waxman?"

"We both know who does them."

Abe laughed even as he tried to focus on what was happening.

"Anyway," Jacob continued, filling the space. "It doesn't matter at all to me whether you do them as part of a firm or as an independent contractor. I don't care. What matters to me as your *friend* is what you'd be able to reach for with the cushion of guaranteed income."

"You keep talking about opportunities and I'm having trouble following."

"So," Jacob continued, "you have people who are interested in helping you. Aaron Goldberg, for example. He said it was great to talk to you, liked your insight. He even told me that he watched you that first night. He said you are a genius with the wood chips."

Which was a thing to hear. Abe felt like he'd lifted a few feet off the ground. "He liked my wood chips?"

Jacob nodded. "He said you were innovative. Not exactly those words, but they come to the same thing."

"Wow."

"Not just wow," Jacob interjected. "He wants to talk to you. Not sure about what, but that's for the two of you to decide."

Mr. Goldberg wanted to talk to him.

Holy crap.

"And then there's Chana," Jacob said as he changed lanes and drove up, past 59th Street.

"Chana? You mean Caf and Nosh Chana?"

Jacob nodded. "She's a spitfire of a woman. Also has a great business, but she's let it slip a few times in front of Anna and I that she's interested in expanding into meat, you see. Can't do it at Caf and Nosh without changing everything…"

"She'll lose her dairy certification, right?"

"Got it in one. Which means to expand into meat, she'll need either a partner or someone who'd be interested in running a second restaurant under her. Possibilities. Directions. There are many. People willing to teach you. Like I told you. Both experience and learning is there for the taking."

As Abe tried to figure out how to respond, and more importantly how to deal with all of this, Jacob pulled over. There was Isaac, lanky, tall, his coat tight to his shoulders.

"Thanks, by the way," the other man interjected as he took a longing look at the front seat before opening the back door.

"You're making me drive in rush hour. You owe me."

"You are saving my tuchus, which I appreciate, but I had to come in to Manhattan. I feel like my passport is expired." Isaac paused, looked at the two of them. "I doubt you'll move your seat for me?"

"I have no idea how this thing works," Abe informed him. "I'm terrified if I touch the wrong button I'll eject myself into the sky."

"And that would be a problem on multiple levels. Don't risk it," Isaac said, shaking his head sadly as he got into the back of the car. "It's fine. I'll just sit in the middle and avoid the *mischegas*. So," he continued, "did you tell him he's back in?"

The noise Jacob made could have been attributed to multiple things, and because Abe was trying to figure out what was going on, he missed what Isaac said. "What?"

"I was getting there," Jacob said, with a sigh of what had to be frustration. "You won the people's choice award, which was a thing even Batya didn't know about. Where's your car?"

Why was Jacob asking him where his car was?

"At the train station? Why? Why do we need my car?"

"I'll drive you to the train station, I'll follow you to your house, I'll take your space…"

"On my driveway? Why?"

"Because you know the backroads of the town better than I do, which means you can get to the theatre faster. I'll

279

park my car in your driveway and then you drive us to the competition."

"Why do we need me to drive us to the competition?"

"You won the people's choice," Isaac interjected. "You're supposed to come back and be the people's champion, representing Rivertown in a way you haven't done since high school."

If the two of them didn't stop, Abe wasn't just going to climb the walls but also out of the window. "Okay wait. Stop the show, not the car."

And in the sudden silence, Abe wasn't sure whether to be relieved or scared. But it didn't matter. This wasn't about Isaac and Jacob or whatever was going on between the two of them. "Now could one of you, and honest to God I don't care which one, possibly tell me what the hell is going on?"

"You're back in the competition," Isaac said. "Which means you're representing Rivertown."

Abe's eyes widened. "How is that possible?"

"Apparently, in every single competition George Gold's associated with, there's some kind of last-minute unexpected challenge," Jacob answered. "This one had a people's choice. The people there, in Rivertown, watching night two in person, voted you back in. Which means you need to let me take your space and then get us to the theatre as fast as you can, so that you can make it back on that stage in time."

Abe nodded. "Now this makes sense. Complete sense." What he was going to do about it was another matter entirely.

"I have to tell you," Isaac interjected. "That I am obligated as Sarah's boyfriend to point out that if you don't fix the heart you broke, there will be serious consequences."

"Jacob and I already covered the fact that I need to be clear and figure things out with Batya."

"Someone listens to me," Jacob said with a laugh.

"Because you're right," Abe replied. "You haven't wavered on the fact that I need to be honest with her and myself about what I want. And make it clear that what I want is her."

"Wonders never cease."

"But most importantly," Abe said, feeling a renewed sense of determination, "I'm going to win that competition."

And Abe wasn't surprised, not even a little, that when Jacob turned on the sound system, the first song that played, was by his favorite band from New Jersey.

Chapter Twenty-Two

L ESS THAN AN hour before the final night of competition, Batya was getting nervous.

Well.

"Where the heck is Newman?"

Linda's voice echoed in the background, her shoes clicking against the tile floor. She was talking to someone, and Batya was glad it wasn't her.

And even if Linda had been talking to her, the answer she'd give would be honest yet heavily censored. She didn't actually have firsthand knowledge of Abe's whereabouts beyond the text Jacob had sent her, telling her he'd found Abe at the office.

What she did know was that Jacob had to drive from the financial district to Rivertown in what was approaching rush hour. Not to mention stop wherever the heck Isaac had decided to ask for pickup. And then fight through traffic before arriving in Rivertown, driving through town in order to deposit Abe at the competition.

And that wasn't even accounting for Rivertown traffic or whether Abe would be in any fit state to compete. Which meant all she could do was wait.

And that was the hardest part. Especially as she was by herself, just backstage.

Worried.

"I'll do this if I need to—the fake people's champion."

She turned only to look in Artur's eyes. How the man had managed to get himself backstage, now, was beyond her. But he was there, and he was a friend and she grabbed on to his gallows humor like a lifeline. "Thanks," she said. "But I don't think they'd let you."

"I was Abe's sous chef in the first round," he said. "I'd be at least filling the space where Abe couldn't appear."

She raised an eyebrow. "I don't know whether that'll bother them."

Artur nodded, looked around them as if he was surveying the scene, though what he was looking for she had no idea. "Trade secret. Live television shows don't like blank spaces. They'll take me up on it, and I'll make a joke, but I don't think it'll be necessary. He'll get here."

She'd ask him how he knew that, or how he'd come to that information. Any of it; the secrets, the trade, before she remembered he was in crisis communications. To her, Artur was the slightly subtle, slightly ridiculous friend with a sour cream obsession that she'd known forever, one of Abe's best friends and her quiz bowl buddy. He was also the PR professional that people called to fix their problems, and he was very, very good at his job.

"Are you sure?"

He nodded. "For what it's worth, he's always loved you."

How did she react to that? Not now, for sure. Later. Much later.

"And yes," Artur said, shaking his head. "I shouldn't be telling you this because he's never managed to express it or help you when it counted, but here it is. And if he screws up again tonight—"

"I don't care if he screws up," she said. "I just want him to show up. That's all."

Artur nodded. "Fair enough. Though I am glad that whatever happens with you two will be post crush."

She paused. What was he saying? "Wait, what?" Her time of analyzing anybody's meaning was over. "I don't get it."

Artur ran a hand through his hair. "The crush you've been harboring is dead, which, I have to say, is good. Because crushes are dangerous. Being with someone is hard work, and crushes are the worst obstacle."

"I'm confused."

"You have to think about this," Artur interjected, pushing past her confusion. "You need to see him as he is, now and always. Whatever happens needs to happen because you see him as an actual adult, a dude with problems, not your dream catch. And I'm not talking about this as a friend of his. I'm talking about this as a friend of *yours*. I've heard you talk about him for years, Batya. He's not your perfect sunbeam, no matter what happens."

No matter what happens.

That was the key, right?

Batya blew out a breath.

"Five minutes," Dr. Engleman said as he approached. "Everything okay?"

Artur nodded. "Yes, Dr. E. Everything is hunky dory."

"Oh, Mr. Rabinovich. You are always there with a joke when I need it. We are, however, missing a contestant."

"Don't television shows have the opportunity to provide a stand-in?"

"A stand-in." Dr. Engleman laughed. "That is the most ridiculous idea I've heard all night. The last I heard, you almost managed to burn down our people's champion's smoker."

Batya shook her head. Small-town gossip struck again. "But we have to do introductions, and we have to point out the contestants."

"I can explain," Artur said. "Because I just got a text about five minutes ago that they were almost here."

"Who's they?" Dr. Engleman asked as the sucking pressure in Batya's chest started to ease up.

"I can stall," Leo said as he came into the room. He was breathing hard, as if he'd run the whole way. "I can give an extensive introduction, make up some excuse about how I messed up a fact yesterday and give a talk about Italian Hanukkah traditions, or you know, maybe tonight's person can do an introduction? Maybe give them more time."

Who was…wait.

Sarah.

Of course she would. If Sarah knew what was happening, she'd definitely help and give Jacob more time to get Abe to the venue.

As her mind continued to race, Artur raised an eyebrow. "Where are they, Leo, and please don't tell me they're on the cross Bronx."

Leo laughed. "Cross Bronx knows not to thwart a man on a mission."

Batya snorted. "I'm almost afraid to ask."

"You should be afraid," Artur said, trying desperately to hide the shudder. "That man—"

"Which one?" Dr. Engleman asked.

"The one who helped me get here in just the nick of time."

Abe.

He was here.

She held herself back, as if her arms were tied to her sides. The last thing she could do and the thing she wanted to do most were the same: run toward him and throw her arms around him as if her life depended on it. It took every single bit of her energy not to do anything other than nod and say "Good."

"I was going to have to cook." Artur smacked him on the back of the head, taking the attention away from her.

"Listen," Abe said to her, ignoring everybody else in the room, "we need to talk. There are words I need to say to you, just you. If you'll let me."

Batya nodded, fighting against every single bit of her willpower. "After this is over, after you do this, we'll talk."

"After *you* do this," he said.

"And that," Dr. Engleman said with a grin, "is how you do it, kiddos. Get into places."

ABE WAS BACK. And he was going to win this thing, not just because of his own dreams and desires, but also because of the group of people who'd made sure he had a chance. Batya had sent Jacob to get him, and Jacob had talked some serious sense on the way over. As had Isaac, for all the man's griping.

But that wasn't all. He could tell as he headed over to his station that Artur had gotten his supplies; his second food processor, the ice cream scoop and all of the details they'd used that first night. Including a wrapped package that smelled like hickory and cherry. And an apron which, when unwrapped, said, 'I love you a latke.'

He was going to win.

His friends deserved it. The people of Rivertown deserved it.

Batya deserved it.

And in the moments between his arrival at his station in

the Rivertown Theatre, and the beginning of the night's competition, he organized himself, grounded himself, and waited.

"Hello, everybody," said an unexpected and extremely familiar voice. "My name is Sarah Goldman, and I'm the chair of Hollowville's Hanukkah Festival. Tonight, I'm not here as the chair but as a fan of the holiday. I love latkes. So much. But here's the thing. All you need to make latkes is a root vegetable, a binder, and some onions. And some oil to fry the mixture in. Over the last few years, people have experimented with different root vegetables, making latkes from many different things. Your job tonight is to choose one of these alternative latke variations and make them yours."

He made his way to the beautiful display of root vegetables set up at the front of the stage. He chose a few turnips before heading back to his station and back to work Just like he had before, two food processors, some quartered apples in one.

Olive oil in the pan. For Batya.

Breadcrumbs in the mixing bowl, also for Batya, as well as eggs. The second food processor on, with the turnips he'd chosen. And stirred like his life depended on it.

Once the mixture was right, he used the scoop to move the batter into the pan. Three judges, two tests.

He did his best, and that was the most he could do. All he hoped was that she saw that everything he did was something she taught him.

THIS TIME WHEN Batya watched Abe step in front of the judges from backstage, she wasn't terrified but excited. He'd done the hard part and even used the same latke recipe they'd made together at her house.

Her house.

Where they'd acted like adults, happy and excited.

Her heart exploded in joy as Abe told the judges he was happy to be here, representing the people of Rivertown like he had all those years ago during the quiz bowl tournaments.

She smiled as he explained he wanted to earn their trust, even if he didn't manage to win, and if she hadn't been impressed by him already, she definitely was then.

"Thank you, Mr. Newman," Dr. Engleman said. "Thank you for competing, and thank you for doing your best."

"It means a great deal from you, sir." Abe said as Batya held back tears she wasn't allowed to show.

As Abe left the room, her heart exploded in happiness. She was so proud of him, so excited for him. No matter what happened. He'd tried, taken the opportunities he'd been given. He was okay.

More importantly, she couldn't wait to tell him so.

ABE DIDN'T GET the competition fairy-tale ending. He didn't go from eliminated to champion, but that was okay. He'd taken a chance and moved from fourth all the way to second, finishing behind the owner of the Kosher Taco truck he'd met in class.

It felt *good*.

Because he'd put his food out there. And when the worst had happened, on national television no less, he was reminded by his friends, his community, and his inner circle, that he was supported, that he mattered.

After the show ended, the winner having been given his prize and his moment in the sun, Abe knew it was time for him to take another chance.

He needed to find Batya. That made his palms sweaty, his fingers shake.

But he headed through the crowds, schmoozing and catching up with people as he searched for her. Finally, he found her. She was in the middle of a group of people, some of whom had to be the production team and George Gold's assistant.

She was radiant. Relaxed and so very, very confident. It was...powerful.

She looked up to see him, and she smiled in a way that lifted him off the ground.

"I can come back," he said, "if you're busy."

"We're done," the assistant said. "Call me?"

Batya nodded. "I will," she said before stepping away and

letting him lead her to the spot where they'd spoken the night before.

He didn't waste any time. "I'm sorry," he said.

"For…?"

"You. You built me up so high that I wasn't ready to think about what that meant, and I got scared. Lashed out at you, and you were the one who believed in me. I'm sorry." He looked down before looking back up at her. "You have always burned so much brighter than you let yourself believe, and I'm just a guy terrified of his own shadow."

"I don't burn bright," she said, taking a step forward, a step toward him. "Not without you."

He raised an eyebrow. He didn't know what to think of the look in her eyes.

"I've always thought of you. You make me feel safe, and maybe that's what I didn't want to let go of, all these years. I was looking for a safe place, and I never found one. But when I came back here, I realized that the safe place I wanted was a person."

He didn't even blink. "I'd love to be your safe place, the place where you come home to each night, the place where you can let the world go. I'd like to try, because in the end what this comes down to," he smiled, "is that I've always had feelings for you, Batya. I'm the worst at expressing them, but I've had them. I've felt them."

"I'm willing to try, but only if you don't shove your dreams aside. Because you've never been that guy. You have options, so many options. And you have, now, the possibility of chatting to someone who can help you figure them out. When you're ready."

Abe nodded. "I'll be ready for anything with you by my side."

And with that, he kissed her, the taste of joy and energy burning brightly in his blood.

Chapter Twenty-Three

One year later

THE HOLLOWVILLE HEBREW Center was full of lights.
Bright.

There was also groaning from the sides. Someone—
though Batya figured Isaac was behind all of it—had managed to get a large, immense, humongous metal menorah
inside the building and turned it into a chuppah frame.

"How the heck did they get that thing in there?" she
asked as she stared at the wildness of it.

"Practice," a familiar, loving voice, said with a laugh.
"Practice."

She snorted, turned to see Abe standing there, noncha-
lantly in a blue sweater with a large Jewish star in the middle.
"Ahh," she said as she put her arm around him. His snorts
and his sense of humor were signs of home these days. "Best
line ever."

Then she realized what he was pointing at.

Isaac had made the frame for the chuppah out of two
menorahs. It was metal, overwhelming, and perfect for them.

"Speechless," she said with a smile. "That is something."

"Something, all right. Didn't think he'd top the books."

The chuppah frame Isaac had made for Jacob and Anna was formed from two books, pages separated from the others. A masterful work of art.

She felt Abe's arm go around her, and she leaned in, trying desperately not to melt. There was too much to do after they set up the synagogue.

"Too early to think about what we'd want, hm?"

She smiled. "You barely gave me keys to the house, much less plans for the theoretical restaurant you haven't admitted you're ready to start."

"So you're not ixnaying the possibility of there being a time when we might need a frame of our own?"

"I notice you skipped right past the whole 'not admitting you're ready to start a restaurant' thing. Which, fine, kudos for your focus."

There was a pause, and she didn't think he was actually going to answer her. There would be words in the space, but most likely not the ones that she was searching for.

Then his grip tightened, just a little bit as if he was seeking reassurance. Because he was. Saying the words meant he was committed, saying the words meant he was going to take the financial leap. "It's going to be a restaurant. I'm looking at spaces. I have a meeting with George next week. To figure out what it's going to be."

While she'd started the show she'd always wanted, he'd spent time learning—a third of the year working with Chana at the Caf and Nosh, a third of the year working with Aaron Goldberg at Goldbergs on Long Island, and a third of the year working with Katie Feldman's Helping Hands project, through a connection Jacob had yanked very easily and very excitedly. She'd shared all of these moments with Abe, and it had been the most fulfilling year of her life, in all of the ways that counted.

She watched him blossom as they both took charge of their dreams.

Now his year of experiences was over. Now he had to decide what he wanted, and she couldn't wait to see him shine. "Do you know what you want?"

He nodded, smiled at her. "You," he said. "You. Forever and always."

And though that was the Abe answer she'd been expecting, it still was sweet. "I love you," she said.

"I love you too," he said. "We deserve our happy ever after."

"We do." And when he turned to kiss her, the taste of the latkes he'd eaten, the sweet applesauce and the unique feel of him, and the wolf whistles in the background reminded her of the most important things in life.

Love, and latkes.

The End

Want another Hanukkah romance? Check out Sarah and Isaac's story in *Miracles and Menorahs*!

Join Tule Publishing's newsletter for more great reads and weekly deals!

Sign up here!

Author's Note

This book started from the smallest gem of an idea; I'd seen so many different Christmas cooking competitions, both fictional and real, and I wanted desperately to see a fictional Hanukkah one.

There had been discussions with authors about different barbecue traditions on social media, and so this is my entry into that conversation as well. Sending extra love and hope to Farah Heron, whose Halal barbecue book I want to read and to Uzma Jalaluddin whose descriptions of biryani poutine makes my heart sing in so many ways.

Guy Fieri's recent documentary about the effects of the pandemic on the restaurant industry, and his efforts to give back inspired George Gold's dedication to the restaurant crisis in his hometown.

When you talk about Jewish food, I think about chefs like Michael Twitty, Molly Yeh, Duff Goldman, Jake Cohen, Jamie Geller, Andrew Zimmern and Joan Nathan, and so many others who strive to tell the stories of Jewish food as they see it. Their knowledge inspired me. And Batya.

Ari White and Izzy Eidelman wrote the book on kosher barbecue. Their dreams, and their ideas inspired and informed Abe's own ideas and recipes.

A random conversation with Lorelie Brown while *History of Us* was being proofread led to my emphasis on Jacob's need to pay taxes. That conversation created the plot space for Abe's day job.

The statistics Jacob cites are sad and unfortunate, but put a few choice words in a search bar and you'll see the evidence of how hard it is for kosher delis to stay in business. Part of the problem is gentilification, when Jewish food traditions become new and just fascinating enough to be swallowed up and homogenized by a food culture that doesn't know why our food works the way it does.

So many recipes for hamantaschen, for example, are consistently messed up by mainstream food outlets by adding butter...because these pastries are supposed to be parve-able to be eaten with both milk and meat. See *Bon Appétit*'s[1] 2015 disaster. And let's not forget about the baker on the famous British baking show who added milk and butter to a challah recipe, and said it was, for, of all holidays, Passover.

Michael Twitty, Carly Pildis and Stephen Wade have initiated serious discussions about how Ashkenazi food developed and why it is the way it is on social media and I adore each of them for it. Michael and Stephen's threads both inspired Anna's lecture and reminded me of why I was doing what I was doing with this book. Carly Pildis's 'Tweet

---

[1] Bon Appetit Magazine Edits Hamantaschen Article to Be More Respectful of Jewish Culture, Purim | Jewish & Israel News Algemeiner.com.

Your Shabat' hashtags bring joy every Friday.

Moshe doesn't exist, but places like Grow and Behold do. They sell kosher pastured meat and explain on their site what that means.

Both Molly Yeh and Guy Fieri hosted Hanukkah food competitions in the last few years. Guy Fieri's *Grocery Games Delivery: Hanukkah* competition gave me special joy during the depths of the pandemic and Molly Yeh's *Ultimate Hanukkah Challenge* opened doors I never thought I'd see open. Both of these competitions inspired the framework of the Rivertown Latke Fry-Off.

Acknowledgments

This was the second book I wrote during the pandemic, written from February to April 2021 and revised from April to June 2021. That I managed it was something I still don't understand. Preparing for the release of *History of Us* and then writing this around the same time was a juggling act you learn.

BUT!

Wordmakers

Two sessions of Lyssa Kay Adams #30 Day Drafters, along with a few extra sprints from Morgan Routh, Kelly Ohlert, Michelle Asmara, Kristin Smith Skees and a few others.

My Tule sprint buddies: Nan Reinhardt, Fortune Whelan, Jadesola James, Sinclair Sawhney, Liz Flaherty and Heather Novak and our twice a week sessions (more when we needed it).

Felicia Grossman. Handholder, cp, friend, all of those don't manage to convey how lucky I am to know you and to be your friend. You are amazing. <3

Lisa Lin: we've been on this wild journey together for a while. I cannot wait to see your name on a book cover, my friend <3 I'm so excited for you and what lies ahead for you.

<3

Michelle Lawson, Mel Ting and Sara Rider: the three of you are always there to yell about hockey, share encouragement and just be there when the chips are up...or down. I cannot wait for our retreat. <3

Hugs and encouragement from the schmoozers—all of you amaze me and I'm so so glad we have our space for each other. *Kol ha kavod.* You all have my heart. <3 We're doing this together as a brilliant kaleidoscope of a writerly *mishpacha.*

My Sunday knitting crew. Our two hours are precious. Our friendships even more so. Thank you. <3

Scott Rosen, Sabrina Schmidt, Devon Wambold, Roxanne Wasiluk: it's been a year where we've been separated but in contact virtually. Sharing virtual concerts has been fun, but I'm looking forward to seeing you all again in person soon <3 And hoping I have by the time this is published.

Joe Fortunato: thank you for answering my questions and showing me how you barbecue. Your setup directly inspired Abe's. Peter and Marnie McMahon were also amazing help, teaching me the specifics of a pellet grill and the joy of what pellets could do when smoked.

Jordan Dabney. Hilary Monahan, Peter Lopez, Shayna Goldman: thank you for sharing your talents and your time with me and with history. <3

Emma Barry, Adele Buck, KD Casey, Jen DeLuca, Felicia Grossman, Farah Heron, Ron Hogan, Piper Huguley, Jadesola James, Melonie Johnson, Bea Koch, Geri Krotow, Liz Lincoln, Angelina M. Lopez, Jeannie Moon, Nicole Moon, Vanessa North, Hannah Reynolds, Brina Starler, Denise Williams, Preslaysa Williams: each of you made the summer of History a lot of fun. Thank you for coming along on the ride with me. I'm so very lucky to know all of you. <3

To the amazing Jewish bookstagrammers who put together the JEWnish book challenge. It arrived right around the time that *History of Us* did and your encouragement and love for *Miracles* and *History* came at just the right time. Thank you for reminding me why I do what I do, why I write the stories that I do—our stories.

And thank you to anybody who read, loved, recommended and supported *History*, who put me on podcasts, and video shows and let me be on panels and talk at bookstores and libraries, and with book clubs, who created beautiful aesthetics and other posts. Nothing happens without your support, not with *Miracles* and *definitely* not with *History*.

To Meghan Farrell, Jane Porter: Tule not only bought one Hanukkah book from me but *two*. Your support of my stories and your belief in me is humbling. I will always cherish that. I cannot wait to see what we do together next. <3

Julie Sturgeon: working with you throughout this series has been a joy. You make my stories better; you make the words I use stronger. You make my stories sing. Thank you for everything <3 I can't wait to see what our next chapter is going to be.

Lynnette Novak: my career and my stories are better with you in my corner. I am so very, very lucky you are my agent.

Voule Walker: proofreader extraordinaire, friend, provider of inspiration. Our weekend chats have given me life, and I'm so glad you're my friend <3

My New York rogues, my Westchester writers, and my Long Island peeps: all of you bring me so much joy. We make magic together <3

Jennifer Gracen, Jean Meltzer: the Hanukkah queens who've been there through this wildness. We're going to take this year by storm.

To Sandy Carielli and Sara Mangel: I'm so glad this year helped me reconnect with both of you. <3 <3

To Isabo Kelly, Laura Hunsaker, Heather Lire, and Cassandra Carr: I adore all of you. Let's GO EMPIRES :D

To Marnie McMahon and Megan Walski: your friendship has always been my light in the darkness. The turnip latkes are for you <3

To Russ Agdern and Marisa Harford: I love you. Your support is so very appreciated, whether it's random questions about barbecue recipes, where you get your meat, latke making or simply saying I adore your writing and want to pass your newsletter on to someone I know. I will never take your love and support for granted

Elijah – I adore your creative mind. Never let the sheep drive the tractor, and may the mini tow always win the race <3 Love, Auntie Stacey

To Jane and Barry Agdern: miracles, history, love and latkes. Everything I do, everything I am is because of both of you. I love you <3

If you enjoyed *Love and Latkes,*
you'll love the other books in the....

Friendships and Festivals series

Book 1: *Miracles and Menorahs*

Book 2: *History of Us*

Book 3: *Love and Latkes*

Available now at your favorite online retailer!

About the Author

Stacey Agdern is an award-winning former bookseller who has reviewed romance novels in multiple formats and given talks about various aspects of the romance genre. She incorporates Jewish characters and traditions into her stories so that people who grew up like she did can see themselves take center stage on the page. She's also a member of both LIRW and RWA NYC. She lives in New York, not far from her favorite hockey team's practice facility.

Thank you for reading

Love and Latkes

If you enjoyed this book, you can find more from all our great authors at TulePublishing.com, or from your favorite online retailer.